To: ▓▓▓▓▓▓

From: Regina Herrera

Re: zombie emergency

Importance level: HIGHEST

The situation is worse than we realized. I've broken into the ▓▓▓▓▓▓▓▓▓▓▓▓ headquarters to see what they're hiding, but I need your help. Get here as quickly as you can. There's something I need to show you. Something you'll only believe if you see it with your own eyes . . .

Scan the code to get started. We're all counting on you.

D1087918

ZOMBIE SEASON

JUSTIN WEINBERGER

SCHOLASTIC PRESS / NEW YORK

Copyright © 2023 by Justin Weinberger

Endpaper photos © Shutterstock.com

All rights reserved. Published by Scholastic Press, an imprint of Scholastic Inc., *Publishers since 1920.* SCHOLASTIC, SCHOLASTIC PRESS, and associated logos are trademarks and/or registered trademarks of Scholastic Inc.

The publisher does not have any control over and does not assume any responsibility for author or third-party websites or their content.

No part of this publication may be reproduced, stored in a retrieval system, or transmitted in any form or by any means, electronic, mechanical, photocopying, recording, or otherwise, without written permission of the publisher. For information regarding permission, write to Scholastic Inc., Attention: Permissions Department, 557 Broadway, New York, NY 10012.

This book is a work of fiction. Names, characters, places, and incidents are either the product of the author's imagination or are used fictitiously, and any resemblance to actual persons, living or dead, business establishments, events, or locales is entirely coincidental.

FOR DAD: THANKS FOR READING ME
THE HOBBIT THAT ONE TIME.

FOR MOM: THANKS FOR GETTING ME
THAT TROMBONE.

THIS IS YOUR FAULT.

PROLOGUE

DUSK ALERT: Take precautions immediately. Emergency conditions exist throughout Marin County, Sonoma County, Lake County, and Mendocino County. Mandatory evacuations are in effect. Throughout Dusk, flashpoints may arise without warning. Flee to safety.

By the time Lucy Santifer's mind caught up with her body, she was already halfway out of bed. Her phone was alive with the emergency warning they'd all been taught to fear—*DUSK ALERT: Take precautions immediately . . .*

The phone repeated its warning, the urgency hammering her and making her heart jump in her chest. She mashed the buttons to silence it, but this time, it wouldn't stop blaring. Something clicked and she realized: The blaring wasn't coming from the phone. It was the sound of sirens outside. Sirens so loud, it was like they were right in the room with her.

Beyond the window: movement.

Lucy looked out and saw exactly the thing they were being warned about.

This wasn't a drill. This wasn't in some other town.

It was really happening.

Here.

Now.

"MOM!" she shouted. She grabbed the go bag from under her bed. "Dad?" she said, barely recognizing her own voice—it seemed so small and far away. The sirens deadened everything.

She looked outside again.

Focused.

Lucy Santifer could not account for how much time passed as she gazed out her bedroom window. A second, an hour, an age of the world—there was no way to keep time, no way to wrap her mind around what she was seeing. A wave was moving across solid ground. Raw, abnormal bodies pressed tight against one another, clawing over one another. Tumbling down the steep, scrubby hill toward the house she'd lived in all her life, engulfing everything in their wake.

Lucy had seen zombies before. But being face-to-face with an entire, unstoppable sea of them . . . it was different. It . . .

"It's okay, Lucy," she heard her dad boom in his deep voice, outside her door. "We're heading to start the car."

"Okay, Dad," Lucy replied. But it wasn't okay.

The zombies were close. Too close.

Underneath the blare of the siren, she could hear them. That garbled roar, like a world being devoured.

She shook. All her muscles, like she had no control over her body.

Stop it, she told her body. *You have to go.*

From the table next to the bed, she snagged a framed photograph. She stared at it, seeking strength. Wishing her friends were here and grateful they weren't.

Hopefully they were safe.

Unlike her.

Tears stung her eyes. Why had her family stayed?

Her parents hadn't thought the threat was real.

And now . . . the Dusk was coming for them.

"Lucy?"

She turned, and saw her older brother, Bo. There was a look in his eyes she'd never seen before.

Total terror.

"You okay?" he asked in a shaky voice.

She nodded, grateful to Bo for finding her. For getting her out.

The car outside honked. Their parents were yelling for them. Bo guided her toward the front door as the hill behind the house disappeared underneath the surging bodies. Hundreds of undead monsters hit the house like waves crashing on a sandcastle.

The windows exploded inward.

Lucy realized she couldn't hear any sound after that. The scene played on mute, like there was no air, in slow motion.

The phone, still clutched in her hand, vibrated. She felt it, and without looking, knew it was the normal first text of the morning from her best friend. She couldn't read it, but the words didn't matter at all in that moment. Somewhere, not too far from here, this was a normal morning, sun coming in the windows, and Joule was eating breakfast cereal straight from the box, texting Lucy. Meanwhile, Bo pushed Lucy out their front door ahead of him, window glass cutting his skin.

Lucy's mother screamed for them to get into the car. Once they were in the back seat, she planted a kiss on Lucy's head without looking away from the nightmare that was coming for them.

Lucy turned and stared. It was impossible to look away. The zombies weren't just inside the house—they were all over the orchard. Ripe fruit was trampled, unnoticed. If a tree was in the way, the zombies tore through it. The harvest they'd stayed here to collect, because evacuation meant losing the crop, was destroyed in seconds.

This close, it wasn't a wave anymore. Lucy could see the distorted faces. The burning eyes, reflecting something inhuman inside. The mouths open in a silent pain and an extraordinary hunger. The rotten-egg stench of them was overpowering.

Lucy's dad hit the gas just as the bodies started to stumble into the road.

There were so many of them.

Too many of them.

Lucy knew it was over, with a clarity that her parents didn't. The Santifer family car plowed forward, but the horde just kept coming. Sweeping across the road ahead, cutting off the only escape route.

Lucy's father sped on, plunging into the moaning bodies. Some flew over the car on impact, but others clung on. The car strained but couldn't push forward. In the back seat, Lucy shut her eyes—even behind her eyelids, the flames of the zombies' eyes cut through. An intense heat reached inside the car. She took Bo's hand. She held on. She made a wish, and kept it close. Speaking it would break its spell, so she just held on and held on, as the engine was torn from the hood and the metal screamed.

The last thing she felt was a ray of sunlight on her eyelids, before something awful stole in and blocked it.

1

SEMPERVIRENS

When Joule came to live in the Northern California countryside three years ago, it was the cloud-scraping trees that reminded her most of where she used to live. In New York, looking down from a tall building made her feel like a small part of a big, big thing. Here, it's the reverse. Here, looking up is what gives her the thrilling feeling.

Her father had taught her that coastal sequoias live longer than most of human history put together, and they grow so tall that they collect water from clouds without it ever having to fall as rain. Standing in the middle of a grove of them, it feels like you're above it all. Like it's entirely possible to slip into another world.

Now Joule climbs up a ladder carefully secured to the side of the largest tree. "*Sempervirens*," she utters. It's the Latin name for these coastal sequoia evergreen trees, and translated it means something close to "always alive."

"Dad?" Joule whispers into a smartwatch on her wrist. "You out there?"

There hasn't been an answer for over a year. But that doesn't mean Joule will stop asking.

Two, three, four. Joule hunches forward, looking through the cracks of the treehouse her father built for her. It's too small for her now. She's taller than some adults, which makes them think she's way older than she is.

She talks into the tiny watch, knowing that its twin is on her father's arm, and that his walkie-talkie function was always on, in case she ever needed him. "I know you're out there, Dad," she says. "Please. Come home."

Joule glances at the treetops, which are now catching orange smoke instead of clouds . . . bringing something that isn't rain into the quiet grove.

Here they come, Joule thinks.

She cranes her neck and sees a flicker of movement that makes her pull back in surprise. "Who's there?" she barks. Only silence follows, and the words ring in her ears.

"Dad?" she says.

A twig snaps.

She looks out, waiting for any sign of movement.

"It's me! It's Joule!"

No one answers her.

That's not him, Joule.

She finds an unexpected trickle of sweat running down her back, and the air suddenly feels too close. She knows how quickly a flashpoint can form.

Like everyone around here, Joule has seen her share of disasters, both natural and unnatural. She's fully aware of how quickly everything can change.

Joule already lost one best friend like that. A wave, out of the blue.

She will never see Lucy again.

No one needs to warn her she should slip away right now. Kids aren't allowed out unsupervised after Dusk has fallen, she knows. But if her dad is here, too, then she's not unsupervised, is she?

After what her mother just told her, she's got exactly zero time left to find him.

"Come on!" she says into the watch, letting caution drop away. "Nelson Artis, this is your daughter! I need you to come home." She feels panic welling up inside her. "'Cause if you don't find me soon . . ."

In her mind, Joule sees the luggage all lined up by the front door of her house. *This is not a discussion, Joule*, her mother told her. *I'm not going through it all again. There's nothing left for me in Redwood. Or for you.*

Joule shuts the door on that memory. Hard.

"I'm not leaving 'til I find you," Joule whispers amidst the trees he taught her to love.

She's waited numbly all year for the Dusk to fall over Redwood and for zombie season to begin. It's a fresh chance to start looking for her father, who found himself too far from shelter last summer, when a flashpoint formed up in the hills—

Missing, presumed dead is what they call it.

Almost a full year without her dad. A fall without anyone texting her funny animal videos to watch on the bus home from school. A winter without anyone to sample her latest baking experiments—like the cherry cayenne brownies Joule made last Valentine's Day. Joule's mom uses her gluten allergy as an excuse, but they all know that she doesn't have a taste for her daughter's wild creations. But nothing made Joule's dad happier than digging into one of her kiwi peanut butter pies, or taking a delighted sip of her signature peppermint coffee milkshakes. Sometimes, Joule would forget—just for a moment—that he was gone. She'd pull a cake out of the oven and take a breath to shout "Dad!" before remembering that the house was empty. Wherever her father was, he couldn't hear her.

A gust of hot air blows straight in Joule's face, and its smell flips her stomach. The orange smoke streaming into the grove gives the green trees a horrible, blood-colored cast.

She forces herself to look straight to the west, where a sole figure crests the hill amidst the failing light.

It has a human face, but its eyes are large and orange. Tigerlike. There is an intense heat coming off it, like the shimmering air coming off asphalt in the summer sun. It has the same pollutant smell.

None of this is a shock to Joule.

Silently, she waits. *Is there only one of them?*

She waits a bit longer, looking around for other zombies.

She knows she should run. She doesn't have a chiller with her—she can't even get a permit to carry one until she turns thirteen.

Don't let it see you, part of her screams.

But another part is asking, *What if it's him?*

"Hello?" she says, trying to make out a face from her perch in the treehouse.

It ignores her. It's focused on scooping leaves and branches into its mouth. It finds a wasp nest in its path, and pushes the papery mass into its face. The insects living inside it try to respond to the shocking destruction of their home—flying, stinging, swarming—and the only reaction from the zombie is a single, small cough. The superheated breath kills all the wasps it touches, instantly.

Joule watches it happen, filled with distress. She sees now it's not her dad. But what if he's out there somewhere, like this? Compelled to consume. Hunger the only feeling inside him.

She's been told a million times, *They're not people, Joule. Even if they used to be. They have no souls. No humanity.*

But Joule still can't bring herself to accept this. "How do you *know* that?" Joule asked her teachers. Her friends. Her mom. And no one ever had an answer that made sense to Joule.

So she stopped asking. And almost immediately, people began telling her how wonderful it was to see her *doing so well.* That they were proud of her for *handling things like a grown-up.*

Every time they say things like that, the mask she wears gets a little more permanent; she feels a little less like a valid human herself. A little more numb and robotic. But she doesn't know how to live any other way than the way she's been living: believing. Refusing to give up.

In a world where *no one* knows exactly what's out there, Joule has committed to discovering things for herself. She trusts the ember of hope deep inside her chest, kept where no one else can see it. It smolders with steady heat.

"Please don't leave me alone out here," she whispers into the empty grove.

Near the base of the tree, there's a rustling in the pine needles blanketing the ground. The earth begins to rise in a gently rounding mound. Like a loaf of bread in the oven.

And Joule hears a voice in her head—the voice of her teacher, her mother, her friends—telling her, *It's too close, Joule. Get to shelter, follow the plan.*

But her teacher isn't here.

Her mother isn't here.

Her friends aren't here.

Joule is here. And she can feel her father's presence here, too.

This moment is one of the few times Joule *hasn't* felt alone since his disappearance. She can't ignore that. That feeling of connection? It's a compass that points out the North Star.

The mound of earth inflates even more and starts to crack. A puff of steam escapes the fissure. From under the soil comes a wordless moan. Dirt *flies* as a body pushes up out of the barrow.

The body flops over, like a fish pulled from the river. Limbs reaching, grime covered, coughing up its first hoarse moan.

Joule looks at the summer's first zombie approaching from the hill as the second one, its roving eyes full of dirt, struggles to emerge from its shallow, grave-like hiding place.

"Time to leave," Joule tells herself, even though in her heart she resists. The time to leave was probably hours ago, when the sky started turning orange.

The first zombie still feasts in the distance. That's a good sign—zombies have single-minded focus, and when they are busy eating one thing, they tend to ignore other potential meals.

The second zombie is still coming awake in the world. Joule figures she might have a few seconds before it focuses on its hunger.

If she's lucky.

The treehouse ladder creaks as she calmly and carefully descends.

The heat coming from the second zombie grows more noticeable as she gets to the forest floor. Its back is to her, but she can see it stiffen, sensing her approach.

There is something familiar about the body.

The right height.

The right shape, distorted by zombification.

A watch on its wrist . . .

Joule shivers. She can't help but wonder if . . . maybe . . .

She summons all her courage and says, "Dad?"

When there's no answer, she lingers a moment.

You can't stay, Joule, says no one.

The zombie is listening. Zombies aren't supposed to listen; they are only supposed to eat and destroy.

"If I go home, my next stop is San Francisco International Airport," Joule says. "I'll never be able to get back. Mom will make sure of that."

The silence stretches . . .

Slowly, the zombie turns . . .

Joule screams.

The face is not her father's.

It was never going to be her father's.

No. Even with the amount of flesh that has melted into a horrific frown, she can tell this man was never her father, and is no longer a man.

It's a monster.

A hungry monster.

Its eyes spark when it sees Joule.

Joule spins around and sprints away at top speed. In normal circumstances, she'd run toward the nearest source of water, but in this case she's let it get too close and has started to panic. She plunges into the densest part of the forest, hoping that the branches and everything that lives within them will slow the zombie down, provide it with an easier target.

The newly awakened zombie erupts in a guttural roar, and from the distant trees, there are others echoing it—from everywhere, it seems.

Branches scrape at Joule's skin and tear at her sleeves. A startled squirrel darts away, scared of Joule, and it runs in the direction of zombies, sealing its fate and probably saving Joule's life.

It's only when the smell of zombies is lost on the wind and their body heat no longer lingers in the air that Joule allows herself to catch her breath.

She finds herself laughing jaggedly. The more it hits her how close she came to being caught, the more intense the laughter gets.

In her mind, the zombie's face is vivid and unshakable. And definitely not her father.

It leaves her wrung out, but even more determined.

He is not dead. Or undead.

He can be found.

She can do this.

She *needs* to do this.

Where are you going to go? she asks herself.

In response, all she can hear are the moans of the undead carried through the trees.

2

MANHUNT

"Oh no, zombies," Oliver calls flatly, making a half-hearted attempt to escape a horde of mindless, destructive monsters. He trudges and trots through the big neighborhood park, until he gets caught.

"*Oliver!*" bellows Coach. "What's going on with you today? What happened to that great hustle of yours?!"

Yeah, okay: These aren't *real* mindless, destructive zombies chasing Oliver. They're regular old mindless, destructive human kids, playing a neighborhood-wide game of Manhunt. It's the same idea as tag, but there's kind of a lot of strategy to it, according to their coach. Coach starts the game at the zombie spawn zone, and ends it at home base, which is a safe zone the kid who's running from the zombies has to get to, before one of the zombies catches them and tags them out. He also analyzes everyone's runs, using data from the smartwatch tracker that the "human" carries when they run.

With a sigh, Oliver jogs over to him. "Coach, I really don't see the point in all this. We've been using these same old fields for years. If we're going to be prepared for the next wave of zombies, we should think bigger. Look."

He reaches into his pocket for his notebook. "I've marked the best routes through the whole north side, the ones that cross over creeks and other obstacles. That's what we should be practicing!"

Coach closes his eyes and rubs his temples. "Oliver, we've had this discussion a dozen times. This is the official protocol. I appreciate that you want to help, but you're just making this harder on everyone."

"But, Coach," Oliver starts to protest.

Coach raises his hand to cut him off. "Not now, Oliver. We need to get back to work. Give it another try." He turns away and blows into his whistle, producing a piercing whine that makes everyone clap their hands over their ears. "Back to your stations!"

Oliver lets out a long exhale and slowly heads back to his designated starting line. Manhunt is a neighborhood tradition here, and it happens every night after dinner. At least until the Dusk curfew officially begins, when it's no longer safe to be running around outside alone. Tonight is a bigger than usual group of kids playing Manhunt, because curfew could be announced any day. This could be their last taste of freedom for a while.

It makes Oliver itchy just thinking about getting cooped up inside again for another Dusk, which gets longer and longer every year, it seems. He's still not recovered from all the anxiety of last summer.

It's exhausting for him to even think about. During zombie season your whole mind has to be ready for a sudden unnatural disaster to strike at any time. You always have to know the closest zomb shelter, the quickest path to a sizable body of water . . . because during an unnatural disaster there can be no hesitation. No questions. When the sirens go off? You grab your go bag and *move*, full stop.

And yet. That's all on top of the rest of being a person.

There's still homework waiting.

There's still dirty dishes to do.

There's probably a scary emergency alert blaring on the phone.

So this time, Oliver flies forward, his heartbeat matching his footstrike, a steady *beat-beat-beat* driving all thoughts from his head. If he can't convince Coach to listen to him, he might as well enjoy the chance to run. For Oliver, running is pure and joyful, and every moment has a simple clarity that it so rarely has when he's sitting still. As he keeps a close eye on the places that Team Zombie might be lurking, he notices one of the "zombies" is hiding in the trees to one side of the path ahead, but he grins and spins away into the hushed wilderness.

―――――――

Standing side by side in the grassy Spawn Zone, out of breath, Darlene Reiner and Chanda Cortez just listen to Oliver Wachs's footsteps echo back as he sprints away. A silence begins to knit together around them as they linger, catching their breath.

"I mean," says Chanda, low and quiet.

"Yeah, I know," Darlene agrees. "No chance we're catching *that* speed demon."

"None. I'm exhausted just thinking about it."

"Maybe Oliver has a point. It's not exactly realistic, is it? Especially when you and I are playing the zombies."

Coach bellows even louder, so everyone who has scattered across the field can hear him: "Come on, guys! It's almost zombie season, act alive out there!"

Chanda shivers. It might just be a game now, but there's no denying that zombie season is horribly real. She looks around the woods and thinks of their best friend, Joule Artis. Joule should be here enduring this humiliation, too—or else on a one-way flight to New York—but nobody knows where she is now.

Meanwhile, Darlene has heard Coach's shout as well. But for her, this exclamation summons up a memory of the girls' *other* best friend, Lucy Santifer, and the awful flashpoint that hit her family's farm. The memory haunts Darlene, even a year after the Santifers were found in their car among the trees they gave their lives to care for.

As Darlene and Chanda stand there, a silence pools around them, like water in a leaky boat. Uncomfortable. Unwelcome.

Chanda braces herself as her brain brews up a terrifying vision of Joule getting turned into a kid zombie, forever eleven years old and eating rocks. "This sucks, wanna bail?" Chanda asks quietly.

"Coach'll kill us," says Darlene, fighting back the memory of when her parents came into the bedroom to deliver the news that something awful had happened to her friend Lucy.

"Chanda! Darlene! Let's move, ya lazy zombies," Coach calls out.

Darlene and Chanda look at each other. The silence grows.

Chanda coughs to scatter it. "Look, here's the thing, Darlene. If Manhunt was a video game, Ollie would have the all-time high score. By a mile."

"By a country mile," Darlene agrees. "Are miles different in the city?"

"Dunno," says Chanda.

"Chaaaanda Chaaaanda!" bellows Coach.

"Are we in the city or the country?" Darlene adds.

"Darlene Darlene Darlene Darlene!"

"We hear you, Coach!" says Chanda, without moving an inch.

"You two are why humanity is doomed!" Coach shouts, finally giving up.

"Should we play the game?" Darlene nudges quietly. "For Coach."

"I guess. For Coach."

Darlene grins. "What's our plan, then?"

"Well," says Chanda. "What if we just go to the place we'd least expect to find Ollie Wachs, and just kind of . . . hang out?"

"Like, wait for him to walk into our trap," Darlene agrees, waving toward Coach and giving him a thumbs-up.

"Isn't that just smart strategy?" Chanda presses. "We're not bailing on the game."

"Man. Joule would have the perfect dumb place to go," says Darlene.

"Joule is *great* at being dumb," Chanda agrees.

"So great."

"And just when you think she can't be any dumber?"

"There she goes."

"There she goes, running away from home right at Dusk."

"Right at Dusk!"

"We *could* go look for her."

"I mean, *that's* truly the dumbest thing imaginable."

"Which makes it smart, right?"

Darlene and Chanda look at each other.

———

Oliver can always keep one step ahead of the other kids. But it's not because he's faster than anyone. It's because of his notebook. The result of long years' work, constantly exploring the town of Redwood and the wilderness surrounding it. Over a lifetime, his notebook has slowly transformed into a really cool, super detailed map. It marks all sorts of secret pathways through the town and shows obstacles known only to Oliver.

Actually? There are hundreds of different scraps of paper in a shoebox under his bed, too, and dozens of different experimental maps, and many, many old stuffed-full notebooks. But in the front of every notebook there is a new and improved version of his masterpiece—or maybe "his *mapsterpiece*"?—that reminds him of all the hidden features and secret pathways he's found in his hometown.

He moves with confidence, pressing through rows of bushes where they obscure passages from one yard to another. Running through the gullies where the rain collects—they're dry now, of course.

But halfway through an empty lot full of tall grass and chirping insects, he skids to a stop, face-to-face with a small girl who has Oliver's brown eyes, blond hair, and pale skin. "Kirby? Are you okay?"

She just stands there. Hands caging something between them.

"Kirby, you're in the middle of our game right now."

Kirby suddenly spreads her fingers, and a huge thing flies out from between them, right toward his face.

"Ah jeez, what the heck!" Oliver cries out.

It's a grasshopper, he realizes, as he watches it fly away and land head over heels in the grass.

His sister grins at his reaction, looking very pleased.

Oliver looks around, at the grasshopper-filled empty lot. For just a whiff, Oliver is reminded of a summer when the sky wasn't quite so orange. When Oliver used to hunt for grasshoppers with Kirby, after school, on the hill outside the library while their mom was inside working. When they used to find crayfish and salamanders in the little stream tumbling through the seam between their neighborhood and the next development. Before the Haywood Wave ripped through, leaving the water and land scarred, and making way for the new development up on the crest of the hill above. He'd forgotten all about those sibling adventures—and as he treasures the memory, a grin bubbles up on Oliver's face.

Kirby grins back.

"Here he is!!" a voice cries out. "Ahhhh, gotcha!!"

Oliver returns to reality too late to avoid being tagged by one of the "zombies," who also happens to be Oliver's best friend, Del.

"Oliver Wachs, your Manhunt reign is over!" Del says, with a tremor of excitement in his voice. Del isn't very good at Manhunt, so it's doubly exciting for him to catch his pal.

"Thanks a lot, Kirby," says Oliver. "I'm dead now."

"Aren't you the one who keeps saying this game is a waste of time?" Kirby asks, rolling her eyes in patented Kirby fashion. Oliver swears his sister learned to roll her eyes before she learned to talk.

"It's better than nothing," Oliver says, though he's not sure whether he believes it.

Kirby flops to the ground and begins to play with the daisies that erupted with the spring warmth. She plucks a few and starts to weave them into a chain, humming to herself. Just as well, Oliver decides; the daisies will wither anyway after the Dusk blocks out the sun. Oliver feels something in his chest twinge. Despite the sass and the eye rolls, Kirby is still a little kid, but because zombie season grows longer and longer each year, she's had even less of a childhood than Oliver has.

Del's eyes go back and forth from Oliver to Kirby. He clicks his smartwatch walkie-talkie twice, sending the signal out to everyone else that he caught the human. Zombies win. In the distance, a loud whistle pierces the uncomfortable silence. "Zombies win. Bring it back in, everyone!"

———

At the same time that Del tags Oliver, Darlene and Chanda are far out of bounds, tracing Joule's usual haunts—specifically, they are surveying the beautiful treehouse her dad built for her.

They don't notice Coach blow the whistle . . . Nor do they notice that there's someone out here, standing in the shadows, watching them.

"She's *definitely* been up here," says Darlene, from the treehouse pedestal above.

"And if this isn't a dug-up zombie hiding place down here, then the apocalypse ain't real," says Chanda, inspecting the disturbed patch of earth amidst the gnarled roots at the base of the tree.

The figure in the shadows shifts.

Darlene frowns. "Did you hear something?"

———

In the shadows, Joule Artis stands very, very still, pretending she's not there, as Chanda and Darlene both peer into the woods, following their usual careful zombie-identification-sweep protocol.

Joule watches as her two best friends give one last look around before a voice emerges from the watches on Chanda's and Darlene's wrists. "Hey, Chanda. Darlene," says Coach. "You guys aren't zombies anymore, come back and huddle."

Chanda and Darlene exchange wordless glances before Darlene breaks the silence. "I don't think she wants to be found."

"I guess not. I just hope . . ." Chanda trails off, her voice cracking.

Darlene takes her hand and squeezes it. "Me too."

Joule wishes she could run over to them and give them a hug.

Why don't you? says a voice in Joule's head.

Because they'll force me to go home, Joule thinks. But what Joule's friends don't understand is that there *is* no home without her dad.

Joule might be hiding in the woods, but she's not running away.

She's trying to find her way home.

3

THE EVENT

Regina Herrera is haunted.

By the zombies that nearly killed her.

By the mistakes she made.

By the day she ruined everything.

It hits her all the time. At school. Late at night. No matter where she is, what happened lives inside her. All she has to do is close her eyes and she remembers racing down a switchbacking California mountainside on a one-wheel, motorized skateboard. Skidding around the tight corners on the gravel road, she looks ahead and spots the mouth of an abandoned gold mine a short distance below.

Well, it used to be abandoned.

Stop, Regina tells herself now. But she can't undo the past. She can't prevent herself from seeing that there's a bustle of activity in front of the tunnel. Dozens of important people, all in suits and fancy shoes on this very hot day.

"Welcome to California gold country!" a woman's voice blares from the speakers set up for today's big event. "A hundred and seventy-five years ago, the discovery of precious metals made right here in these mountains changed the course of our community. But we're not here to talk about the past, of course. We're here to talk about the future."

Regina rushed here from school, as fast as she could, but she's still going to be late. "Come on, pal, gimme a little help," Regina mutters, looking down at the giant rubber tire jutting up through the deck of her skateboard. Its treads whiz by, right between her firmly planted feet. Her heavy zombieproof jacket stays stiffly in place, too, with its Project Coloma patch catching the light, a badge of honor that few people are lucky enough to wear. "Just a little faster," she urges the skateboard.

For most kids, making the miles-long journey from Redwood for the unveiling of Project Coloma would've been impossible. But Regina isn't most kids. She's a Herrera. Just like the woman whose voice is filling the air all around her, Dr. Celeste Herrera. Also known to Regina as Mom.

"What we're here to talk about today is something that's much more precious than any metal." Dr. Herrera's voice echoes off the mountains. "Here in this abandoned gold mine, we've found *hope*."

Regina thrills at the impact of these words.

Get 'em, Mom! Regina thinks. She wants to cheer and clap—

But then she spots a side path down an even steeper part of the mountainside and she puts all her focus on making this shortcut count. *I'm coming*, Regina promises her mother, as she swerves, fearlessly, down the straight, steep path.

The Herrera family has been part of the Coloma Project since the beginning. It was actually *Regina* who came up with the idea for what's now been built here, in fact: a machine that uses zombies to make electricity.

It was four years ago, when Regina was only eight years old. Dr. Herrera was working from home during a zombie wave, and Regina was home, too, because school was closed for zombiefighting. And out of nowhere, Regina asked a question that changed the course of the world, and inspired every-thing happening today: *What if we could build a big treadmill that the zombies all walk on, and use it to make electricity?*

Look what happened, she marvels, gazing down at the mine. And from this high angle, she can just see the glint of sunlight reflected off metal inside the mineshaft. It's not gold, though. It's aluminum and steel. A brand-new structure that's been built, which extends deep into the earth, through the old tunnels. Seeing it makes a shiver go down her back.

"In most of the world, people dump their zombies in places where they can't escape, like Alcatraz, and Yucca Mountain, and right here in this historic gold mine," says Dr. Herrera. "There are over three hundred miles of mine tunnels under our feet, and inside them are countless zombies, trapped where they can't hurt anyone. We make very sure that there's nothing to eat, in most zombie sequestration sites like this, so they can't possibly escape again . . . but down here, we give them *just* enough fuel to keep moving. Fuel that you and I would call trash. Pollution. And the zombies eat it up, like they try to eat anything in their path. And when they try to escape—to climb toward the surface, in search of more fuel—this facility turns their movement into useful electricity, like a river harnessed by a dam. With enough zombiepower, we could light up our whole planet . . . *and* help heal the environment, too."

Hearing her mother say these words, Regina's entire body fills with an incredible, electric buzz. Regina is so hugely proud—of her mother, of herself, of the company behind it all, HumaniTeam. Regina flips down her clip-on sunglasses and leans forward, knowing it'll decrease her wind resistance—which will help her go a little faster.

Today's exciting, but really, she can't wait for *tomorrow*. When everyone finds out what's been secretly going on right here under their noses. Regina can't wait for the kids at school to hear about this. She's never been the most popular kid before. Okay, that's a bit of an understatement. She's actually quite unpopular. "Intense," "scary," and "weirdo" are how her classmates generally describe her.

But that'll change when the rest of the kids start to realize the reason behind Regina's constant annoying questions in class. And her hot embarrassment over getting one answer wrong on the homework. And her endless stream of notes excusing her from school early so she can go do independent study with the team of geniuses Dr. Herrera leads . . . A note that her nervous mother forgot to write today, by the way—which is why Regina had to stay in school until the bell rang and then race like the wind all this way.

Regina feels she'll be living proof to all the other twelve-year-olds of Redwood, California, that their voices are important. That any one of them could be the key to solving the zombie apocalypse. *The future is finally here*, she tells herself.

Distracted by this elation, Regina doesn't notice the giant hole in the middle of the rough trail ahead of her, disguised by a thatch of broken branches and sticks.

There's nothing but thin air and darkness under her board.

The ground opens up, and she falls . . .

4

HOLES

Everything's out of Regina's control. She can only watch as she tumbles into darkness.

Then the moment of free fall slips past her. The electric-white shock of hitting the ground jars her bones and teeth. From the back of her brain, an instinctive panic builds to an avalanche. Time lingers in that emptiness for a terrible moment, Regina's mind splintering in pain, and then . . .

Adrenaline surges through her. Air that was pressed out of her fills her lungs again.

Her mind comes back together into one piece.

She feels a wetness spreading, soaking her clothes. She's in a shallow pool of water, a splashing noise tells her. It's knee-deep as she stands up.

In the distance, she can hear moans.

She has landed inside the zombie facility. Their prison.

She is the newest inmate.

She lights up her phone's flashlight and sees that there's machinery all around her. Cables and tracks and metal scaffolding to support the tunnels and keep the zombies contained. *I'm inside the generator*, she realizes.

Regina recognizes this place from the blueprints she's studied: This is the part of the machine that stores the generated energy and sends it out to the world.

But . . . there's something not quite right. The noise is too loud. It's like a crowd at a football stadium, if the football game was being held in a creepy, darkened series of tunnels underground. She also sees flickers of movement in the long shadows of her flashlight. Pressing in, making her throat feel tight.

This is definitely not right.

The zombies should be a half-mile deep. Not way up here. And that sinkhole she tumbled through—could they have gotten out?

Her mind races.

How many?

Where did they go?

Regina takes a calming breath and forces herself to slow down and think.

Craning her neck, she looks up toward the hole, twenty feet above. Not easy for someone to climb.

And there wasn't any evidence of zombie activity aboveground, either, now that she thinks about it for a minute.

If some zombies got free, it'd be extremely hard to miss the proof of their presence, because they'd've started devouring everything in sight. The woods would be stripped. Nothing but dead sticks. So that logically means the zombies didn't escape. For a moment she's relieved.

But then she realizes that if the zombies haven't escaped, that means they're still here.

She watches the shadows very closely for any sign. Any movement.

Above, Regina hears her mother's amplified voice reverberate eerily through the cavern.

"On behalf of all of us at HumaniTeam, I'm proud to show you the Naturally Regenerating Generator! Let's start the tour."

"Hello?" Regina calls out, and the echoes bounce everywhere. "Mom?!"

No one answers her.

Regina pulls her skateboard out of the water and watches it drip. She taps a message on her phone, searching for a signal. No luck.

Regina starts to feel very alone at that point.

She also feels a sudden heat prickle on the back of her neck.

Slowly, carefully, holding her breath, she turns around.

Behind her, there's a figure. Another kid. A boy, with pale, dirty skin. About the same age as Regina—but with eyes like a tiger. Fierce, dazzling—and . . .

Orange.

Zombie-colored.

The prickle of heat on Regina's skin grows fierce. She can't move. She can't breathe. This is it. A part of her has always wondered how she was going to die, and now she knows.

She dies today, right now, trapped underground with a zombie.

Its mouth starts to open, and it's like campfire smoke hits her square in the face. The sensation is just enough to shake off the numbness that's taken hold of her.

Regina spins around, willing her legs to take off in a sprint, but the boy grabs hold of her jacket sleeve. She feels the unrippable, zombieproof material jerk her to a stop in her tracks. His warm breath singes her skin again and a cry scrapes its way out of her throat. Is this the last sound she'll ever make? A moan of despair?

No, she thinks as the zombie pulls her closer. Screams of pain will be the last sound. Death by zombie isn't a peaceful way to go.

A surge of anger burns through her terror.

This isn't how it ends for me.

With a furious strength that Regina didn't know she had inside her, she lunges forward and manages to escape the zombie's grasp.

For a second, the zombie boy seems confused about how she escaped. Then he reaches toward her again, stretching for the tail end of her long coat.

Regina shrugs her shoulders, slips out of the coat, and sprints away.

She turns a corner and sees two other zombies blocking her path, walking in lockstep toward her.

Regina looks around for anything that she can use to help her escape. In a facility like this, there's no shortage of the world's most advanced zombie-fighting equipment.

Sure enough, she sees a gently glowing red emergency light, marking the nearest superchiller. It's just a few feet away. She smashes the glass with her skateboard and pulls out the chiller, grasping its tank and aiming its nozzle.

It's not a moment too soon. Both zombies rush to meet Regina. One dives and grabs her ankle so tight she can feel an immediate bruise.

The other goes for her head.

All the preparedness drills kick in. Regina unleashes the superchilled water inside the extinguisher right into the upright zombie's open mouth. The noise it makes is both a choke and a roar as it stumbles back, its flesh solidifying into a lifeless shell that's dashed to pieces when it hits the ground.

The zombie at her ankle yanks hard and the chiller falls from her hand. She can feel the zombie's grip crawl up her leg. Now its mouth is opening, eyes aflame—

This is the part that haunts Regina the most.

It is the moment she ran out of options.

The moment she gave up.

And then—

The zombie is toppling over, hit from the side. Someone else has tackled her attacker, putting their body between her and it. Regina looks up to her savior.

It's the boy. The zombie boy.

The zombie boy's mouth slowly opens, a sound emerging.

"Run!"

Regina still doesn't know whether she heard the word spoken or if it was just in her mind.

She grabs hold of the skateboard and throws it down in front of her, helping give it a jump start. Betting that its motor still works.

Focus up, let's go, Regina tells the skateboard. *You and me can do this, pal.*

Turning to look back, seeing the zombie boy staring after her, she shoves her phone in her front pants pocket, flashlight angled so it works like a headlight, and jumps on the quickly rolling board. For a second, it does nothing. Then it leaps to life, zooming down the tunnels.

She is not alone.

Horrible faces flare in the red glow of the skateboard's taillight, jaws wide, eyes haunting. Moaning. Hungry. Tireless in their pursuit, confident in their defiance of all who would cage them, including death.

Regina's mind races as fast as the wheel on her skateboard. *Which way?* she asks, depending on memory of only a blueprint to guide her.

The tunnels fly past, one after the next, and she tries to find the confidence she had just a minute earlier. She digs deep, but it's not there like before.

On the back of her neck, her dark hair stands on end, and her ears twig with the feeling of being followed, chased—*hunted*.

Finally, she sees the pale glow of the emergency exit in front of her.

It's an armored elevator, with an alarm box that can set off a powerful sprinkler system to soak the zombies throughout the whole mine. She'll be safe once she's there.

But the sprinklers will wipe out the generator's ability to produce electricity, too, because it'll neutralize all the zombies.

As she zooms ahead, the elevator door seems to anticipate her arrival somehow. It dings, and opens, bathing the tunnel in clean, bright light.

Inside the elevator, Regina finds a crowd of adults. The whole tour group, led by her mother. Regina takes in the horror on their faces, as they see her.

As they realize what's chasing her.

"Gina?!" her mother asks in disbelief, barely a whisper.

"Mom!" she calls out, racing into the elevator.

Regina barely slows the skateboard down before she collides with her mother, squeezing her tight as the door closes with a clean, pleasant *ding*.

For a moment, nobody breathes.

A security camera on the wall shows a group of zombies in the corridor outside the elevator.

"Oh no," says Dr. Herrera. Taking in the situation. Thinking fast.

Regina sees her mother glance around at the other adults in the elevator, while reaching for the emergency sprinkler system trigger, arming it.

In the back of her head, Regina knows that pulling the alarm means that this is the end of Project Coloma. Regina feels her stomach turn sour.

"Mom, wait," says Regina. "Don't pull that switch. We can fix this. It's—it's—"

Outside the elevator, and everywhere else in the zombie-filled mine, the sprinklers all hiss to life at Dr. Herrera's signal.

This is the truth Regina will never escape: It was all her fault.

Her mother's company managed to cover up the scope of the breach. The wider world thinks there was just a delay in the project.

But even if it can be erased from the news, it can't be erased from Regina's memory.

She can't stop thinking of the zombies who almost killed her.

She can't stop thinking of the zombie boy who might have told her to run.

5

THE ZOMBIE BRIGADE

The inside of the Redwood Zombie Brigade Headquarters is a really cool place, full of actual zombiefighting equipment and actual zombiefighters. No one here would mistake eleven-year-old Oliver Wachs for such a heroic person himself, but he crosses the wide-open, cavernous main hall like he belongs there, passing a long table filled up with cadet candidates who are all at least five or six years older than he is. All around him he hears the sound of pencils scratching on paper.

"What's going on in here?" Oliver asks, stepping up to the sign-up desk at the front of the room.

"Taking a test, kid," says a man behind a name placard that says PROCTOR.

From across the room, a woman in a stiff, zombieproof coat, wearing a superchiller pack on her back, calls out, "He's with me, Harold! He's here to help with my YouTube thingy."

The sight of Chief Carrie Wachs makes Oliver smile. "Hey, Aunt Carrie!" he calls back to her.

"Hang tight, Ollie. I'll be there in a couple minutes."

"Chief, I can't babysit right now," says the proctor behind the desk. "We're doing a new recruit evaluation here today."

"So evaluate him," says Chief Wachs.

The proctor looks coldly at Oliver from head to toe, and Oliver smiles. Oliver sucks in his stomach, standing as tall as he can, his sun-freckled skin flushing with self-conscious nerves. "I don't need a babysitter," Oliver says, even though he's suddenly feeling like he's very small.

The proctor hands over a packet of essay questions. "Good luck."

"Thank you. Can I borrow a pencil?"

The proctor looks annoyed, but hands Oliver a dull, wooden pencil with a chewed eraser.

"What's that in your pocket?" the proctor asks, pointing at the beat-up green notebook in Oliver's butt pocket.

"This?" Oliver takes it out, holding it in the careful way that only the son of a librarian can. "Just a notebook. Actually, a map. Actually, I should show you. It's awesome. I use it to—"

"Leave it on the table," the proctor says.

Oliver deflates. "What?"

"You can't have any notes during the test, that's cheating."

"Oh. But—"

"You wanna be in the brigade?"

"Can I?"

"No. But if you want to be a brigadier when you're older, you need to start acting like one and listen to your superiors without asking a zillion questions."

"Why?" Oliver decides that he doesn't like this guy very much.

"Why? Because following orders is how people stay not dead."

"People not staying dead is kind of the whole problem with the world, though," Oliver snarks back. The words are out of his mouth before he realizes it.

The proctor glares and points to a sign that says NO TALKING DURING THE EXAM.

"'Kay, whatever." Oliver glares, slaps the notebook down on the table, and heads to the closest open chair.

As he looks back up at the proctor, he sees the man has his grubby hands all over the notebook, snapping its pages back so hard they almost tear. Oliver feels a hot fury blossom inside him, but with heroic self-control, he manages to focus on the test.

"*What is the Dusk?*" the first question asks.

Oliver rolls his eyes as he writes out an answer.

Dusk is when the sky turns red during the summer. It's caused when huge hordes of zombies kick up huge clouds of dust and ash that hang in the air for days or weeks at a time.

Anyone who can't answer that question is lucky to be alive, Oliver tells himself, flipping over the sheet of paper so fast he gives himself a paper cut.

"*What is a flashpoint?*" the second question inquires.

"Oh, come *on*," he mumbles, sucking on the web of his thumb where he got cut.

A "flashpoint" is the term for a zombie swarm that can arise without warning during the Dusk. Sometimes, if there's not enough fuel around to feed it, a flashpoint can disappear on its own, but most of the time a flashpoint grows and grows until it turns into an unstoppable zombie "wave," and then they give it a name, like it's a hurricane. Oliver gains more and more confidence as he writes. *Like any unnatural disaster, a flashpoint is a really dangerous emergency. The best way to stay safe in a flashpoint or a wave is to follow all evacuation orders right away, no matter what.*

Is this really all it takes to get into the brigade? Oliver turns the page again, and reads question three. *"How are zombies created?"*

Oliver sighs and scribbles the same non-answer he's written on countless tests in school.

There is currently no consensus to explain why some deceased humans are reanimated as zombies and why some are not. Burial practices around the world vary, but they do not seem to affect the size or frequency of zombie flashpoints.

"Why do zombiefighters use absolutely pure water to fight zombie hordes?"

Oliver hesitates a second, until the answer bubbles up from his memory:

Zombiefighters need totally pure water because just like zombie blood is super-heated, pure water can be supercooled, so that it stays liquid way below freezing. And that means that it's way more powerful for fighting zombies. It actually turns to solid ice when it hits something. Water from the faucet or a river can't do that, though.

Oliver shakes out his cramped writing hand as he reads the next question: *"Describe the scientific process for creating water that's pure enough for zombiefighting."*

Oliver's pencil goes very still, poised over the paper, as Oliver's mind is perfectly blank.

It's complicated, Oliver writes, and then, without looking back, turns the page.

"What is the history of human-caused climate change and how does it attempt to explain the existence of zombies?" Oliver is completely stumped. He's starting to understand why the pencil eraser is so chewed up.

"What are the four substances in the body of a zombie called?"

He feels himself starting to sweat, like he does when he eats cheese too fast, and goes to flip the page over to the next one—

"Yellow bile, black bile, phlegm, and blood," a familiar voice whispers in Oliver's ear.

Oliver looks up at Chief Wachs. "Thanks, Aunt Carrie," says Oliver. But as he starts to write them down, she tugs him away.

"This way, pal," she says. "Thanks for helping me out today, by the way. It's much less annoying making these videos when you're on the team."

"Anything I can do to help," says Oliver, feeling a little bit sulky.

As they approach the front desk, Oliver deposits his test with the proctor like it's a toxic substance and snatches back his notebook with the green cover. As Chief Wachs leads Oliver away from the evaluation area, she sees his frustration.

41

"What's wrong, Ollie?" she asks.

"What does it even matter what's inside a zombie? What's important is stopping them."

"Stopping the zombies means understanding the world around us."

"Come on, Aunt C. Isn't it a little bit ridiculous that I'm supposed to live in a world where zombies show up without warning, but I'm not allowed to fight them?"

Chief Wachs thinks a moment, and then she says, a little more firmly, "If you want to be in the brigade one day, learn the four humors that make up a zombie's body."

"Yellow bile, black bile, phlegm, and blood," Oliver parrots back instantly.

"Yeah, fine, I deserved that. So then, what role does each of them play in a zombie?"

"Aunt Carrie . . ."

"Yellow bile and black bile are related to why zombies are always hungry and devour everything in their path," says Chief Wachs. "Phlegm is pretty much a synonym for snot, which is just gross and takes up space. And blood?" She pauses, with a raised eyebrow.

Oliver smiles and answers, "Zombie blood is where the energy is stored. It keeps them from getting tired. It's superheated."

"Which means what?"

"Superheated blood is so hot that it normally boils away like water on the stove, but when it's inside a zombie's veins, it stays liquid. Even at a thousand degrees."

Chief Wachs smiles at Oliver. "Good. You've earned a prize."

"Really? What?"

She hands him a giant empty trash bag.

"What's this for?" he asks.

"You should be recording this, Ollie." Chief Wachs nudges him.

Oliver takes out his phone and points the camera at her.

"'Kay, you're on."

"Hey, folks, we're *live* from the Redwood Zombie Brigade Headquarters. I'm Chief Wachs, and I'm here to make sure everyone has the tools to stay safe this summer." She brandishes the nozzle of the superchiller on her back as she says this, but then she looks at the nozzle in surprise. "Oh, wait. My bad, wrong hand," she says, stowing the nozzle and pulling out a big black garbage bag instead. "Hey, folks, I'm Chief Wachs, and I'm here to make sure everyone has the tools to stay safe this summer."

She grins at Oliver. Oliver looks embarrassed to be alive.

"Many people, like my nephew, assume that a superchiller is the best tool for surviving a zombie encounter—"

"Aunt C!" Oliver complains.

"—but if you really want to prepare for the zombies this summer, head outside and clean up some trash. If there's no fuel for the zombies, then they'll find someone else to terrorize."

"That's a load of garbage," says Oliver.

Chief Wachs laughs, eyeing the bag, which is an actual load of garbage.

Oliver smirks, just now realizing the joke he just made, but Chief Wachs is totally serious, it turns out. Out behind the big administration building where both the zombie brigade and the emergency call center are located, in a section of woods next to the highway, Chief Wachs and Oliver slowly fill the bag with litter strewn all across the ground, while Oliver records video clips on his phone to make a story. Through it all, Oliver continues to pester his aunt, baffled at her resolve.

"So can I ask a question?" says Oliver.

"Yes, Oliver?"

"Say we pick up all this trash and a bunch of zombies still show up anyway."

"That's not a question. But it's very possible, of course."

"Right, so, here's the question . . . then we better have a superchiller, right?"

"You're just a hammer in search of a nail, aren't you?" the chief says with a frown. "In the right hands, a full bag of garbage is every bit as useful as a C-pack if you're face-to-face with a zombie. More, I think."

To Oliver's disbelief, she continues.

"This trash is more effective than any zombie bait you can buy at the store, Oliver. If you're faced with a zombie, you can just chuck it away from you and run the opposite direction, and the zombie will go after the easy target while *you* run for safety. Truth. Actually, sometimes if the brigade needs to slow down a fast-moving horde, we'll dump a whole truckload of trash right in their path. Did you know that?"

"Did not," says Oliver, mentally making a note. "I do have one question, though."

"What's that, Ollie?"

"If you don't think you'll ever need that C-pack, can I have it?"

Through the camera, she has this picture-perfect flustered look. And at that moment, Oliver calls out, "Cut! Your face was *perfect*, Aunt C."

"Well played, Cadet Wachs."

Despite his best efforts to stay sulky, Oliver beams at his aunt with pride. "I gotta go upload this. It's gonna be a *classic*."

She sighs and shoos him off. "Glad you're on my team, Oliver."

———————

Halfway home, moving along a grassy sloped pasture, Oliver stops to look at a strange new depression in the earth. A hole. Too large to be an animal, it's about four feet wide, and it winds, dangerously narrow, into the rock.

He throws a stone in, and hears it skitter and clack for a long, long time.

It's an odd-looking thing. It goes down and down, and it looks weirdly fresh, too. Peering at it with his keen eyes, he reaches for his notebook to write down the details. But when he sees how late it's getting, he sighs and marks it for further spelunking tomorrow.

6

SANCTUARY

Joule wakes up on the hard ground as headlights shine in under the barn doors. It takes her a moment to remember where she is—the Santifers' orchard. Inside their barn. Next to Joule's head, there's a glowing phone screen. The video she was watching when she accidentally dropped off to sleep continues to play:

"And once you've got the valve fully attached, you can test for any leaks by dunking the whole chiller into a water bath—"

"That's normal water, not supercooled water, ha ha ha!—"

"Good point, Oliver, thank you for that important safety tip."

"Oh jeez," Joule says, immediately silencing the phone. The cringy video has not left Joule feeling great about humanity's chances.

Outside the barn, she hears a car door swing shut. Then a second door. Scrambling to look through a crack, she sees a man and a woman. A radio squawks with voices, heavy shoes grind the gravel beneath them . . .

Police officers? Joule thinks, fighting back a jolt of confusion.

"Joule?" a woman's voice calls out. "Joule Artis? You in there, sweetie?"

Joule tries to hold her breath. She doesn't dare to move. When there's no answer from inside, the man and the woman talk quietly to each other, and then Joule hears them trying to unlock the barn door. Faced with a quick decision, Joule looks around at her options.

Her brain is still sluggish. An uncooperative part of her just wants to answer them and be taken home—it's been painfully slow progress searching for her dad. But Joule knows what that means—within twenty-four hours, she'll be on a plane to New York with her mom, and her dad will be lost forever. Joule's not naive. She knows chances aren't good that her dad is out there. At least, not in any form she'd recognize. But according to the police, he's still *missing*, presumed *dead*, and Joule is focusing on that "presumed" with all her might. "Presumed" means probably but not definitely. It means no one knows. Not really. So how can she give up the hunt? How can she accept the word "dead"?

Silently, she looks through the crack in the door.

They're not police officers, she sees. They're part of the zombie brigade. With heatproof coats and everything. They even have their C-packs on, just in case there's a zombie around that needs to be soaked.

Joule knows it's too early in the season for that many zombies to be appearing.

But clearly, the season has other ideas.

Her eyes move to the antique-looking superchiller that she's been getting back into working condition, using nothing but YouTube videos. On tiptoe, she goes over to pick it up and strap it to her back.

The lock on the door rattles, but it resists all their attempts to get inside.

Eventually, she can hear the footsteps move around to the side of the barn. Then the back.

Here's your chance, says a voice in her head, as she looks at the door. *Go now*, the voice tells her. Holding her breath, she turns the lock, keeping it as quiet as she can. The barn door eases open a crack, just wide enough for her to squeeze through.

You're doing great, Joule, the voice in her head cheers. *Don't forget to relock the door.*

Joule pauses in the midst of walking heel-to-toe across the gravel and remembers the hide-a-key that's in her pocket.

Rolling each foot to keep quiet, she goes back to the barn, right into the bright headlights.

"Joule, honey? We know you're in here, we tracked your phone," someone calls. "You're not in trouble. Your mom is just worried."

With total silence, she relocks the door. She resists the urge to run or look back, keeping as quiet as a ghost, as she makes her way to the nearest line of fruit trees.

Now she's just got to keep still, and she's home free.

"If you want to be home free, all you have to do is tell them you're here, Joule," says the voice in her head. *"They'll take you home, free."*

It's exactly the joke her dad would've made, she imagines, missing him even more. Needing him even more urgently. Out here, in the middle of the night, she just—she needs him back so badly.

For just a second as the brigadiers come out of the barn and slam the door closed, she thinks about calling out.

She feels that little-girl part of her get the urge to rush out and yell, *Stop! I'm here!* To be given a rest. To plead that she's not ready to deal with grown-up problems. With friends dying. With her dad not being around to help her.

Joule has tried to move on, like her mom clearly wants. But she can't do it, because . . . because . . . as her mind bounces off this question, she feels an itch to run away.

She misses him so much.

She thinks about all the things that her father's love held for her. The promise of a world that can grow, wild and free. The course laid out for her, every trail moving with purpose, like a stream runs toward the ocean, deep and full. The laughter that she refuses to let go of.

"I love you so much, Dad," Joule says.

She pulls herself into a ball under the low branches of the fruit trees, and listens, and watches the brigadiers head back into their car. The zombie-fighters' car doors close, and the headlights turn away from the barn, but still Joule doesn't move. She stays there, her back against the tree. She closes her eyes, making no sound.

Pretending as hard as she can that she's one of the trees. Or a bee, pollinating their flowers. Or the fungus growing through the ground, spreading across the whole orchard. She almost feels like she is . . .

The next thing Joule knows, the early morning light is spilling over her. She smells the air that is clean and warm with the new sunlight, and smiles.

The Santifers' orchard has become a place where she always feels close to the people she loves who aren't here anymore. A sanctuary.

She thinks about how hard it was to make it through the night, and she thanks her dad for giving her his determination.

Unlike most people, Joule's dad didn't pretend that he had all the answers. But he always knew how to *find* answers. He could always figure out how to figure things out.

And then she takes a deep breath, willing herself to summon a memory of the man who built her a treehouse using nothing but YouTube videos. That and, like, wood and nails, of course. And tools, sure. And deeper than all that, a determination to give his daughter a place in this world that was hers. That goes without saying. A place that she could climb to, and look out from, and make her own . . .

In her memory, she sees him watching a YouTube video, surrounded by wood and tools, insisting that they will become a treehouse. *Your mom's gonna kill me, but I gotta stick this out and make it work, Joule.*

Joule sticks it out, too.

"Sorry, Mom," Joule says, tightening the straps of the newly repaired superchiller onto her back and heading out, in search of something no one else believes is possible.

7

TRAILBLAZING

"Hey, guys," says Coach, waving and coming toward where Oliver and Del are sitting on the ground with flashlight, a headlamp, and a rope. "Glad you made it to practice early, too. I wanna talk to you about something."

"We're not here for Manhunt, Coach," says Oliver.

"What?"

Oliver gestures to the cave-like opening in the ground that he discovered yesterday.

"Whoa. What the heck is *that*?" Coach asks.

"We're going to check that out," says Del, pointing at the flashlight and rope.

Coach frowns. "But, guys, I need you today."

"Coach, you gotta relax," says Oliver. "Practice isn't everything."

He doesn't relax. "These practices are only useful if you work hard. And as your coach—"

"As my coach, you know I can get past anyone here," Oliver interrupts.

"*Anyone?*" says Del, still crowing about his big win.

"Nice," Coach adds, giving Del a high five.

Oliver always wondered why Coach was so dedicated to training them, and then one day he let it slip . . . the fact that he'd lost his sister and her family to a zombie attack. So many people shared the same story. Trying to tell their family how to prepare. Begging them to leave dangerous areas. And then, once the Dusk had cleared, going in to find that the worst had happened, and there was no way to fix it. Not for the people they loved . . . but maybe for other people, next time.

"I got to thinking about that idea of yours." Coach crouches down with them and takes out the tablet he uses to analyze all the Manhunt games. He taps a few icons on his tablet, and shows them his screen. It's got a satellite picture of Redwood. The busy, main downtown area with the big buildings and grid streets. The leafy north side of the valley with the orchards and sheep pastures and nature preserves. The fancy new moated community that's still under construction—and rows and rows of homes in sheltered, hilly cul-du-sacs: the neighborhood where they all live . . .

"What'm I looking at?" Oliver grunts, intrigued.

He zooms in on their neighborhood on the north side, and as he does, the open spaces and backyards reveal a web of weird, squiggly red lines, like trails. "This is a diagram of the best escape paths you trailblazed this year. I've analyzed the tracking data from every single game we played, and I mapped out five different escape routes you discovered. Paths that anyone can use to escape a flashpoint in our neighborhood this summer."

"Really?" Oliver says, feeling a sudden swell of pride. And as he looks at the screen, he can see each of the trails in his mind, in a way he never did before. In a way that's instantly etched in his mind. "Coach, that's—*really* . . ."

"Incredible!" Del says, taking a picture of the screen. He leans close to the tablet, prodding it with his finger. "We should all get this tattooed on ourselves for safety."

"That's one way to go," Coach says. "*Or*, we could go out today and mark the trails, unless you're too busy for it?"

After a moment, Oliver grins. "I mean, I'm honored to," he says.

By the time the rest of the neighborhood's regular Manhunt players catch up to what's happening, Oliver and Del have already finished marking one of the trails, and they demonstrate to the group to look for all the piles of stones, ribbons around branches, even markings on curbs with nail polish and model paint.

Oliver watches with swelling pride, and thinks about all the other secrets out there still to discover, and to share.

8

DIGGING DEEPER

Regina Herrera has this memory of going to school the day after "the Event" at the gold mine when everything went wrong. Somehow, rumors about the generator's failure had erupted among the kids in her class, stories that were even wilder than the awful, shameful reality.

Hey. You like movies? Regina hears in her mind, remembering one boy's question the next day at lunch.

Huh?

Your T-shirt.

The shirt Regina wore that day used to be one of her favorites, emblazoned with a picture of Arnold Schwarzenegger as the Terminator and the words COME WITH ME IF YOU WANT TO LIVE.

If your parents had ever watched like ONE movie, they would've known it was a bad idea, what they were doing.

She shivers at the memory.

She doesn't wear that T-shirt anymore.

Because what that kid didn't know? Project Coloma hadn't been Regina's parents' idea. It had been Regina who'd come up with the brainstorm to build a generator that uses zombies to make electricity. So. If there was a fatal flaw in Project Coloma, then *everything* that happened is pretty much Regina's fault.

Regina gazes out at the long, low office building through the chain-link fence as she cruises toward it on her skateboard. HumaniTeam's regional office in Redwood. The place where her parents worked on Project Coloma. All those long nights, planning, designing, arguing, celebrating . . . it's all dark now, since the Naturally Regenerating Generator was permanently condemned and Project Coloma got shut down.

It's up to Regina to come up with a solution. A way to fix what she ruined.

Dismounting her skateboard near the chain-link fence, she tips the board up and hides it in the bushes. She moves with practiced ease, slipping inside the fence through a gap no one knows about other than Regina. The guard is the only human being left out here these days, so once she's past them, all she has to worry about are security cameras. And those are easy-peasy. If she couldn't figure out a way to defeat a dumb camera, she'd hardly be worthy of the name Herrera.

As she sneaks through the empty building, punching in the security code to her parents' private office, Regina feels a new flood of guilt, shame, anger, and doubt—all the feelings that she's been trying so hard to keep at bay.

This building ought to be full of life. People coming together to make their dreams a reality. Their big, crazy dreams—like a version of the future where zombies aren't the end of the world. Passionate and brilliant people, working hard, even when everyone's exhausted. Late nights and early mornings. Together, as a team.

It was the greatest feeling in the world, to Regina.

They would've known it was a bad idea. Regina hears that taunting, sneering boy's voice in her mind.

Ever since the incident, Regina has been tormented by the idea that she overlooked the most basic truth imaginable, and ruined her mom's life, and wrecked everything for all the people working here. So here she is, trying to solve the mystery of how it all went so wrong.

Here's the thing, though. Regina still hasn't been able to find any fatal flaw in the Naturally Regenerating Generator. Project Coloma should have worked. Clear and simple. All Regina's research points to this truth.

She asks herself the obvious, mysterious question. *But then how did the zombies escape containment?* Because they obviously did. And she nearly died because of it.

She's gone through everything so many times. And every time she cobbles together yet another arrangement of facts, they don't add up to tell a logical story. There were so many safety measures—there's no good explanation for why the zombies escaped almost the whole way to the surface.

As she thinks back to that day once more, she feels her gut drop. It's the same feeling of falling that she's felt so many times before. Darkness swallowing her, the electric-white shock of striking the ground.

It's a memory, she knows, but it's just as intense as ever.

And one reality is as true now as it was then: Regina is still very alone. She's as much on her own here as she was down in that hole.

More, maybe.

The whole Project Coloma team has been scattered, moved to other projects, including her father, who has been traveling for the company and consulting on a project up in Alaska, and her mother, who is involved in something super secret with the code name Cloudbuster.

Regina digs out her carefully hidden stacks of documents and blueprints. An old iPad she coaxed back to life that's still got a bunch of old emails on it.

Through this careful, silent process, Regina slowly starts to feel kind of paranoid. It's not easy to explain, but when she closes her eyes, she can feel a . . . a presence.

Like she's not alone out here.

She doesn't believe in ghosts or such nonsense, but if she did, this feeling would be a lot easier for her to describe. Instead, she ignores it and keeps working.

"Come on, buddy," she says to the tablet that's taking forever to load up a new email thread about an underground radar survey. She's trying to see if there's any way that the zombies could have burrowed through the ground to avoid triggering the alarms and setting off the automatic sprinklers.

As she waits, she produces an apple from her backpack for an energy boost. It only makes her hungrier. She's suddenly ravenous, for some reason.

Closing her eyes, she takes a second to think like she's one of the zombies. Stumbling through the dark. Following the lead of the others—just instinct, pulling her forward. Moving through the earth, needing to keep going. The power storage area where she encountered them—that would be almost a beacon for a zombie, wouldn't it? Full of raw power that the zombies could use? But there's no pathway to get there. Not that's on her blueprints and surveys, or in any email, report, or Post-it note.

She lets herself slump back in her chair.

And behind her closed eyelids, she feels that ghostlike presence again. Nudging her a little. Not in words or anything. Just a general notion. If you rule out all the possible flaws in the NRG that could allow the zombies to escape, then what does that leave?

"If it wasn't something about the NRG that caused the containment failure," she mutters, "then . . ."

She feels a chill go through her, right on the edge of an unbelievable thought. "If it wasn't something about the NRG that made it possible for the zombies to escape, then what if there was something—what if there was something about *the zombies* that was different?"

Regina's breath catches slightly and that part of her mind that's always working on a puzzle in the background, even while she's asleep, is fully engaged now. She's onto something. In her mind she hears Sherlock Holmes saying his famous line, *When you have eliminated all which is impossible, then whatever remains, however improbable, must be the truth.* In this case, that means: If nothing about the generator was flawed, then the only thing that could be responsible for the zombies' escape from the mine . . . is if there's something strange about the zombies themselves.

Time drifts past, unaccountably, as Regina combs through all her resources, looking for any clues about where the zombies in the mine came from. What waves they were originally part of. But each time she thinks she's found what she's looking for, there's just . . . nothing.

There's tons of data here. On everything.

Everything but the zombies. There has to be a logical explanation, she tells herself. She's just not looking in the right place or something.

Because the other alternative is that someone has removed all the data about the zombies from the files.

Sometimes, the answer you seek only leads to deeper questions.

Something prickles the back of her neck. That lurking presence feels like it's right behind her. Whip-fast, she spins around.

Regina's eyes catch a flicker of movement outside the window.

"Shoot," she hisses to herself.

For a second, she starts to make a run for it. But then she skids to a stop, panting. She needs to know who has been spying on her. This could be the end of her mission, if they tell anyone what she's been doing out here.

A chill settles into Regina's body.

She squats down low, and keeps out of sight as she heads toward the door.

She peers over the windowsill, but from this angle she can't tell who it is. All she can see is the scuffed and slightly tattered heatproof coat.

Before Regina can act, the figure stands up and *shatters the window* above her with an elbow.

Regina recoils as a shower of glass rains down on her. She crawls backward, keeping her eyes fixed on the figure—to her surprise, she sees that it's a boy about her age.

A boy with orange eyes.

And a jaw that hangs open, muscles too powerful to close.

Her heart races as she feels for the door latch, crawling toward safety without taking her eyes off the window.

The zombie climbs through the window, inside the office building. And Regina notices the coat has a very familiar patch on it.

It's a logo for the Coloma Project. It's *her* jacket. The one she lost when—when—

In Regina's mind, slippery, lightning-quick thoughts collide, mixing reality and memory.

She does a double take, not believing her eyes.

The zombie that stands over her is the same zombie she saw in the mine. The one who tore off her jacket, who helped her escape.

How?

When the emergency sprinklers went off, the whole place was doused with superchilled water.

None of the zombies should have survived.

There was no logical way for any of the zombies to survive.

And yet.

Here.

In front of her.

Regina's gaze moves past the boy, toward the window. There are more zombies coming inside. And behind that—there are *dozens* of hard orange eyes peering out at her, from the gnarled trees. Watching. Not moving, not consuming. Impossibly, it's as if they're waiting for a command.

Which makes no sense.

Zombies don't have willpower like that.

They don't work as a team like that.

Whatever remains, however improbable . . . Sherlock Holmes repeats as the zombie with the Project Coloma patch locks his awful orange eyes on her face. Regina feels her throat tighten.

He reaches out a soot-covered hand.

When she doesn't respond, he seems to smile, exposing a set of terrible teeth.

It is too late for her to run.

9

PRESERVE

"If a zombie eats you in the forest, and there's no one around to see it, did it even happen?" Joule asks, standing perfectly still, in the middle of nowhere, alone.

It's not really a joke, though. Not exactly. It's a wish. A bargain with the universe.

And she holds her ground in this wilderness, a mile and a half from the nature center where her father was last seen alive. The flashpoint that her father got caught in wasn't anything famous or notorious. It didn't grow into a wave, so it never even got a name.

But here's proof of its existence.

On one side there are lush greens and rich browns, while the other side is bleached, dry gray husks. It's the place where the flashpoint was stopped. Where the zombies were turned back. And yet it's already regrowing, one season later.

But in Joule's imagination, she can only see the furious, hungry horde, pulling her father in. Carrying him away as their prize. And then—

She pushes away the next image, slapping herself in the forehead to try and focus on why she's out here. "Look, here's what I think, universe. You can just give him back to me and no one will know."

With all her heart, she calls out, into the trees. "Dad! Come on."

There's no reply, not even an echo.

With a heavy sigh and a tiny smile, she lets the wish drift away, into the world.

Then she sees a flicker of movement out of the corner of her eye. Even before she turns to get a sharper look at it, she knows by the sudden heat against her skin that it's a zombie. No: It's more than one. A clump, all surrounding something they've killed.

She's just far enough away to convince herself she's safe. Or at least, not in immediate danger. She forces herself to examine the horde. This is what she's here for. There's no turning back now. But even that knowledge isn't enough to keep the creeping horror at bay as Joule surveys the surreal scene.

Monsters with mouths that open wide like snake jaws, their superheated breath shimmering. With hands that shove anything in reach into those waiting mouths. Trying to eat everything in sight, like a baby does when they're too little to know better.

She lingers, watching. Heart thumping, she searches for her father's features. But all she finds are unfamiliar mouths slightly open, strangers' eyes fixed on their prey.

Joule feels ice in her veins. No matter how many times you've seen zombies in the news or on the internet, nothing can ever really prepare you for such a sight up close. The press of arms and legs, fingers and faces. It's strange and a little alarming to see flares of orange, scintillating—like the lightning bugs Joule used to see, dancing in the purple shade, back east. But *these* hallmarks of summer aren't things you go chasing after.

Except for Joule, of course.

When zombies start to clump together, they attract one another, and before long there's a proper flashpoint. And if there's enough fuel around for all those zombies to devour and keep devouring, then it'll grow and grow until it's big enough to call it a wave, which the zombie brigade will give a name and everyone who was there when it happened will remember, and call it by this name for the rest of their natural lives.

Joule jumps as a voice comes from right behind her: "Can I help you?"

With a sharp breath she spins, seeing a woman with gray hair and a light brown uniform shirt like the park rangers all have, but without any name tag or badge or anything.

"Hello there. Something I can help you with?" says the woman.

Joule immediately gets a creepy vibe from her. The way she stares. Like she's able to see right into Joule.

"No. I'm fine, thanks." Joule blinks, turning back to the trees, searching for the shadowy figure. But all she can see is a poof of dust drifting through a ray of sun, creating a comforting, golden glow. It's like that calm they say is in the eye of only the biggest storms.

"Sorry, I—I didn't know you were even out here. I'm looking for—look, my dad is right over there, I'm fine." Joule's not exactly sure why she lies, but something about this woman makes Joule feel unsafe.

"Oh." The not-ranger lady blinks, her eyes getting distant. Then she looks at Joule with fresh eyes, in comprehension. "So you're *Nelson's* girl."

"What?" Joule's stomach suddenly drops.

"Yeah, your dad's over to the left there. Thaddaway."

Joule feels the blood pump hard in her veins. "Sorry, what?"

"Just keep on heading straight. Can't miss him."

Joule's face goes hot, and even though none of this makes any sense, she rushes off toward the trees where the woman gestures. Heart pounding with a sick, queasy weakness, she calls out with everything she's got, "Dad?!"

There's no answer, though. Of course there isn't—there's no way her dad's just been hanging out at his job this whole time—like it's just been a really long day and he forgot to come home two hundred nights in a row.

She turns around and sees the old lady a short distance away. She's keeping an eye on Joule but also bending over, foraging for something in the dirt.

"'Scuse me," says Joule. "Ma'am?"

"Annette," says the gray-haired woman, plucking something from the forest floor and turning it over in her hand. She brushes it off, and pops it in her mouth. She closes her eyes with relish. "This is the right spot," she says.

Joule doesn't know what to make of that. She looks around.

"Look. My dad's missing. Like I tried to tell you. If he's your friend, you should help me."

Annette looks at Joule closely. "You don't want to find him. You want him back the way he was. That's not how it works." Annette keeps foraging at the base of a tree, and Joule sees what she's harvesting. A beautiful mushroom patch.

Your dad's not out there, Joule, says the voice in her head. *Let's get out of here.*

Joule ignores the voice, though she keeps a safe distance from the old lady. "How do you know my dad?"

Annette eats another mushroom. "He was always kind to me."

Joule isn't set at ease by this. She points at a mushroom. "What are those?"

"Body's gotta eat," says Annette with a smile. "Want one?"

As Joule looks at Annette, she feels a creeping horror. It's hard to explain. But it's enough to send her running.

She runs until she's turned around and not quite sure which way she came from. All she's thinking about is getting away from *there*.

But here isn't so great, either. The air here has a weird haziness, she notices. A slightly yellow cast, like a sickness. There's no lack of zombies out there, Joule knows. What started as a trickle several days ago has quickly gathered momentum. It wouldn't be weird at the height of the zombie season, but this early?

A wave of heat hits the back of her neck a moment later. And then she feels the ground shudder, and a moan rises on the wind. More zombies. Suddenly, she gets that horrible feeling that this might be more than she counted on.

She can feel the heat coming off the bodies. From the mouths, the nostrils, the armpits. It makes an invisible dome that surrounds her like a boa constrictor, squeezing her, so her lungs can't fill. It's so sudden that it almost feels like being swallowed.

And Joule thinks to herself, *If a zombie eats you in the forest, and there's no one around to see it, did it even happen?*

Sometimes the answer isn't worth what you have to do to get it, says the voice in her head.

Weirdly, the warning to leave makes her more focused on why she's out here. What the stakes are. It's about bringing her dad back.

She's waited a *long* time.

An entire autumn, winter, and spring, over two hundred sleeps. None of them particularly restful. Each night when she's asleep, she dreams of him, out there, calling for someone to flip on a light switch that he can't find . . .

How could she leave Redwood like that? Go start a new life somewhere else, while her father is . . . while he's . . . lost in the dark, with no one.

So Joule tightens the straps on her C-pack and stays right where she is, watching the zombies, her eyes flickering from unfamiliar face to unfamiliar face.

There is something a little unsettling about them to Joule, though. She can't put her finger on why right away.

But then it finally hits her what's strange: They're not eating. They're all just . . . waiting.

Waiting for what? As she asks herself this question, something changes. There's a shift in the air, and the zombies all seem to react to a silent signal.

They see something.

Hear something.

Sense something.

Panic rises in Joule, but it's too late. If they turn on her, she's as good as dead.

As one, the zombies charge out of the shadows—

Joule jumps straight back, but the zombies are moving away from her. They ignore everything in their path and charge—ripping past the chain-link fence, charging right toward a long, low office building.

On the other side of a broken window, she hears the sound of a struggle. Her heartbeat rises as she sees a girl her age run out of the building and tumble to the ground, with zombies all around . . .

10

TRAIL, BLAZING

Oliver moves with purpose through the trees, following one of the trails Coach marked on the map. For the first time, it feels like he's finally *doing* something—something that'll actually keep people safe during the next flashpoint.

He can hear Darlene and Chanda coming toward him long before he sees the girls scramble through the hilly, uneven landscape. They're part of the scheme to mark running trails through Redwood, but . . . as usual with Darlene and Chanda, everywhere they go, they find themselves keeping the silence at arm's length:

"I told you I don't wanna argue, Chanda."

"I'm not arguing with you, Darlene. I'm agreeing."

Darlene laughs. "Let's agree to just move on, okay?"

"Okay, but there's no believing or not believing. It's fact. There's evidence of naturally occurring zombies going back thousands of years."

"Here you go with your cave paintings," says Darlene.

"By 'cave paintings' you mean 'ancient hieroglyphics'?"

"I hate you so much."

Chanda shrugs. "Hate me all you want. Mummies are still real-life zombies when they're walking around and not just staying in their tombs."

Darlene is exasperated. "What actual evidence do you have of mummies walking around?"

Chanda ignores this question. "And what about the zombies in the Bible, Darlene?"

Darlene looks horrified, and lets out a frustrated moan. "Chanda, I beg you—"

"And on the third day, he rose again!" says Chanda.

"Jesus did not bust out from a barrow in the summer and rampage through the streets of Nazareth," says Darlene.

"Prove it."

"You prove it."

"YOU prove it."

"Hey!" Oliver interrupts, waving at them as they bluster past where he is hauling stones around and marking a trail section with two parallel rows.

It makes Darlene and Chanda jump.

"*Ollie?*" says Darlene. "Don't surprise us like that."

"I've been here for ten minutes," he says. "Are you two finished marking your piece of the trail?"

Darlene and Chanda look at each other. "Kind of."

"What do you mean 'kind of'?" Oliver asks with a groan. "For once, we finally have a chance to do something useful. So why do I seem to be the only one who cares?"

As the question hangs there, Oliver catches something in the girls' expressions, and he feels himself soften. "Sorry. You were looking for Joule. Right?"

"Well, we're not *not* looking for her," says Chanda, folding her arms.

"Why aren't you? Joule's out here, right now. Alone," says Darlene. "And you think we're just going to forget about her?"

"How about I help you with the trails, and we can all keep looking?" Oliver asks.

"Oh man, that'd be great," says Darlene, perking up.

"Yeah, thanks, Ollie," says Chanda, picking up two rocks and handing them to Oliver.

Oliver sighs, looking at the gap in the neat line of stones marking the trail, where the pair of rocks used to sit.

"Okay, come on," he says, leading them onward.

"Ollie, we already went that way," says Darlene.

"True. But this time someone will actually be paying attention!" says Oliver.

As Oliver takes their part of the trail and figures out how to mark it clearly, Darlene looks her friend in the eye, and speaks softly. "I gotta know. About the zombie stuff—you're just messing with me, right?"

Chanda whispers back, "Dunno, really. I commit so hard, sometimes even I don't know."

Darlene holds Chanda's eye and marvels at her absolute honesty.

"Wowwww," says Darlene. "That's kind of bananas."

"Yeah, I know. I take things too far."

"No, not *that*. I totally respect your commitment to the joke."

"What's bananas, then?"

"I was like one hundred percent, absolutely sure you'd never let me know whether or not you were messing with me. Sorry, C.C." Darlene thinks for a second, then changes her tone. "Whatever, no I'm not."

Chanda Cortez quirks an eyebrow.

Darlene shrugs. "The world is ending, and I'll be honest with my best friend if I want to."

Chanda's smile could be seen from outer space.

Oliver grins, listening to them carry on as he matches up landmarks around him with the map sketches in his green notebook, clearly marking each of them. A path unfolds, step by step.

"So, okay," Darlene says. "*A* country isn't the same thing as *the* country, right?"

"Right."

Oliver's keen eyes catch the glint of something slightly to one side of his trail, and he investigates as the girls tromp onward. "Are we in *the* country right now?" Darlene inquires.

Before Chanda can cook up a reply, Oliver calls out: *"Hey!"*

He's at a crossroads of two paths, looking at something in the dirt underfoot. "Does Joule wear sneakers or boots?" says Oliver.

"Boots," says Darlene. "Big old hiking boots."

"Ones her dad gave her," says Chanda.

"Never takes 'em off."

"Okay, that's what I thought." Oliver gets a sharp, focused look, as he considers something they can't see.

"Ollie Wachs," says Chanda. "Start talking fast."

"Look," says Oliver. "There was a girl standing right here, wearing big hiking boots." Oliver gestures to a patch of dirt by his feet.

"You can tell that from the dirt?" says Darlene.

Oliver ignores the question, pressing forward. "And another kid, wearing sneakers, was here, too," Oliver continues.

Darlene leans down close to the dusty ground, where there are smudgy footprints. Possibly. Maybe. Craning close to the dirt, eyes peeled, examining the ground like it's a page full of words. A story waiting to be read.

"I'm pretty sure it was like . . . two minutes ago," Oliver declares.

Chanda stares straight at him. "Are you messing with us right now?"

"No!" says Oliver. "I found a—"

Darlene looks up. "Wait. He's messing with us?"

Chanda crosses her arms. "Come on. You really believe he's, like, what, some kind of expert tracker?"

"Could be if I wanted," says Oliver.

"Could *not*."

"Stop talking for one second and listen!" Oliver points them toward a gently glowing object just off the path: a phone.

"Whose phone is that?"

"I'm not sure, but look at the photo it just took." Oliver holds the phone up so they can see the picture on its screen. It shows a bunch of different blurry legs, standing right where they are right now—one pair of legs ends in big chunky hiking boots, and the other pair has these new-looking yellow high-tops, like skateboarders love.

"Wait," says Chanda. "How do you know when this was taken?"

"Well, if the screen didn't automatically lock, it was probably just a minute or two ago, right?"

The girls look both impressed and frustrated.

"Which way did she go?" Darlene asks Oliver, urgently.

Oliver looks around, pointing in two directions. "Well, there's a path that way, and a path that way."

"Ollie, come on!" says Chanda.

He points a third way. "There's a path that way, too."

They look upset.

"What? Don't get mad at me," he demands. "You were right, okay? I'm not an expert tracker."

"Hold on." Darlene looks up again from examining the photo. "Ollie? I think you missed something."

Oliver crams in next to her to look at the screen. He sees what Darlene is pointing out. In the background of the photo, there's another, slightly blurry leg in the picture, just on the edge of the frame. And if you follow the leg down, to where it meets the ground . . . there's a smudge there that

74

looks an awful lot like a sooty wisp of smoke curling up in the air . . . and another, and *another* . . .

"Those are zombies," says Oliver.

"Yeah."

"Like a bunch of them, looks like," he says, feeling a shock go through him. "Right here. Where we're standing."

"Uh-huh."

"It can't be," says Oliver. "It's still too early in the season. It takes a couple weeks after the first sighting at *least* before there's enough zombies out of their barrows to reach critical mass."

Oliver feels tension all through his body. Not *new* tension, exactly— because you have to be relaxed to tense up, and nobody ever relaxes in zombie season—but it makes his stomach flip, and his jaw tightens a notch beyond normal as the fading light casts the trees and houses in shadows that seem impossibly deep.

11

EVENING

Regina stares up at the zombie standing over her, frantically searching for something to defend herself with. The boy's face is so close, his warm, putrid breath scorches her skin. Death is a heartbeat away. A bitter taste fills her mouth as memories flash in her mind.

What if it's not a curse? Dr. Celeste Herrera tells the eager crowd in the foothills of California gold country. *What if . . . it's an untapped resource? What if we can turn its destructive energy into power for our hungry planet?*

Here and now, Regina scrambles out the door, crab-walking backward so she can keep her eyes fixed on the zombie. Then she lurches to her feet and runs. Slamming the outer office door open, around the corner, setting off alarms and triggering the motion sensors—Regina ignores it all and keeps moving.

She bangs the emergency exit open and sprints outside. Looking back, she sees the building is being torn apart behind her. Fifty, sixty zombies. The glass and aluminum are no match for their strength.

And the boy zombie in the jacket keeps coming toward Regina.

He's not interested in the building. Or anything else.

He's here for *her*.

Looming over her, his mouth continues to hang open in an unnatural way. Black soot marks his footsteps as he matches her movement, step by measured step. Wisps of smoke curl up from the dry pine needle carpet of the forest, leaving a sooty trail. Regina's restless imagination carries her back again, to the old mine.

In most of the world, people dump their zombies in places where they can't escape, like Alcatraz, and Yucca Mountain, and right here in this historic gold mine.

The audience's smirks offer a clue about what they think of this idea.

Regina blinks away the memory.

The zombie in the Project Coloma jacket's hands move forward. Toward her.

But Regina won't live long enough to puzzle out why, it's clear. Curiously, the puzzle-brain that's always working in the background is more upset about never knowing the answer than it is about Regina's impending death.

She braces herself for what's about to happen as the zombie's hands keep coming down toward her, its fingers reaching.

On behalf of all of us at HumaniTeam, I'm proud to show you the Naturally Regenerating Generator!

She remembers the clapping and laughing—and then . . . disaster.

Regina keeps replaying little fragments of memories, her eyes tightly closed.

The heat in front of her is intense. Overwhelming.

And she feels her heart thud *fast*, very much still alive, somehow.

77

Opening her eyes, she meets the eyes of the monster. They dance with scintillating reflections. Alien and thrilling, unreadable, terrifying.

His hands thrust toward her again and she lets out a cry. *This is the end.*

Only . . . it isn't.

And this time her eyes stay open, so she sees the dirty, gaping mouth with its twitching lips. But they don't seem to be trying to devour her.

The zombie produces a raspy sound, then tilts his head, almost expectantly.

It's trying to talk to me, she realizes, in disbelief. But zombies *can't* speak. Everyone knows that.

"Stay," the monster croaks.

Regina feels her jaw drop.

No.

This is impossible.

"Stay," and then, barely audible, *"Please."*

Regina looks closer at the hand extending toward her. It's not a claw or a hoof. A hand, like hers. There's an intense heat coming off it. And then it opens. The boy-shaped monster is offering to help her to her feet. She has only to reach for him.

Will it burn me? she wonders. A growing curiosity begins to unfurl its tendrils inside her. She doesn't act on it. Not yet.

As she thinks, the monster's heat seems to slowly creep toward her. Evening out, like when you turn on the faucet's hot and its cold, and they mix. After a moment, she barely even notices it . . . which isn't a good sign, probably.

"Nix," the teenager-shaped monster rasps. Dirt-streaked, black-haired, unreadable eyes. *"Me."*

Regina finds herself looking around at the others.

In the woods, the other monsters surrounding her all stare. Regina's eyes go back and forth among them all. The one called Nix watches her closely, his hand still before her in an offer of help.

Regina tries to demand an explanation, get control back on her side in this mind-bending negotiation. But the words don't come.

"You're . . . alone," the monster says. Every word is an effort.

Regina pushes herself to her feet.

"Need more . . . friends . . ." he says, his inhuman eyes flat and unreadable.

Regina thinks about this. Is he saying he needs more friends . . . or that she does?

"I need to go home," she tries to say. All that comes out is, "Home."

"Yes. Home," he says, like he heard her anyway. *"You. Me. Them."*

Regina laughs, wildly. Out of control. He lets his hand fall.

She starts choking, and it turns into a coughing fit. She tries to get air in her lungs, to tell this monster what she thinks of the way it tries to find friends and allies. But every time she tries to spit out the words, her mouth is less and less cooperative. She feels a chill settle deep inside her. She's shivering, suddenly. *When did it get so cold tonight?*

Nix watches her, without a hint of surprise. *"It's not . . . the end . . . of the world,"* he says. *"Your home . . . is with us . . . now."*

A wave of weakness travels from head to toe, like she might pass out.

The monster watches her, with a horrible, awful, patient smile. He tries to make his face comforting, but it's even more awful, in its false friendliness.

That's when a gush of supercooled water strikes Nix in the side of the torso, making him yowl in bitter surprise. The water seems to start freezing and boiling at the same time, and the zombie throws himself to the ground, as Regina turns toward a girl with a chiller pack on her back, its nozzle pointing at the zombie. She has wild hair, like she's been sleeping on the ground for three straight nights. As the two girls lock eyes—

"Run!" the girl calls to Regina.

A wordless scream rips out of Regina's throat with more urgency and agony than she's ever felt in her life.

She turns and *runs*, faster than she's ever run before.

12

9-6-6

"We have to call the zeebies right now," Darlene says hoarsely, still staring at the phone that documented Joule's recent moment of horror.

"This doesn't make any sense," Oliver insists, making a careful zombie identification sweep all around them. "I don't see any signs that there were zombies here, do you?"

"Uh, does this count, Ollie?" Darlene points at the ground.

Oliver follows her finger and gasps. The ground under them is rising like a loaf of bread does in the oven.

A hiding place.

A really big one.

As Oliver watches, a clawlike hand erupts from the center.

"Get back!" he shouts, pulling Darlene and Chanda back as another hand bursts through the dirt like a gruesome, impossibly fast-growing flower.

Then another, and another.

It's a zombie ambush.

Chanda's already holding the phone to her ear.

"9-6-6 Redwood Call Center," a voice says. "This is Lou speaking. What's the situation?"

The earth rises and rises until it splits.

Like a mouth opening wide.

And from this mouth, a dozen zombies are expelled onto the ground, steaming in the moist dirt, which quickly cakes and cracks. It makes them look like creatures of clay as they scrabble over one another and get to their feet.

Oliver is shocked. He's seen zombies before, but always on a horizon, or in the trees.

Close up, the zombies are terrifying not only as a threat, but as a physical presence. It is hard to tell where one zombie's flesh ends and the next zombie's flesh begins. Their limbs are skeletal but seem boneless at the same time. The smell is like a bonfire of burned hair, choking but with a rotten sweetness, filling his nostrils and sticking to the inside. And their eyes— their eyes are the most living thing about them. And also the most inhuman.

"Hi, um, hello?" Chanda tries to speak, but as she draws a breath, she finds the air that hits her lungs is suddenly very hot. It makes her cough, and robs her of the air needed in order to speak.

"Caller? Hello?" says Lou.

Chanda finds she can't answer the question. She looks to Darlene for help, but Darlene is hypnotized, staring into the dark—where two orange eyes meet her gaze—staring, unblinking, on the hunt—and words seems to fail her, too.

"You're not coming through clearly right now, caller," Lou says, sounding very, very far away.

Zombie moans simmer on the breeze.

"Come on!!" Oliver calls out, bounding toward home. "This way! Just like in—like in pruh—practice." Coughing drives the words from his lungs, too, and the sooty heat makes his vision go dim, and full of sparks that are hard to differentiate from the horrible orange fury of those eyes.

"Okay, caller, if you can hear me: We're sending help," says Lou as a keyboard clacks in the background.

As Lou speaks, a dozen more firefly eyes stare back at Chanda, Darlene, and Oliver. From the darkness, more moans approach.

13

NIX

"Run!" Joule Artis calls to the girl on the ground at the zombie's feet, as she opens the hose's nozzle the whole way, unleashing a blast of superchilled water that turns to ice as it hits the body of the monster. It immediately melts again and turns to gas—that's how much heat is in the superheated blood of a single zombie.

It's startling to Joule to watch the monster react to getting soaked. At first, the damage looks devastating—its body gets stiff, and the veins pulse—but just as quickly, the supercooled water is vaporized and the zombie's anger returns with even more intensity, eyes brighter, air shimmering with heat all around it like invisible armor. It's shocking to see how much power there is trapped in that human-seeming frame.

And then, when the C-pack sputters and the water stops, the monster's awful orange eyes lift, and it takes a step forward, tireless and unstoppable.

"Let's get outta here!!" Joule calls out, adrenaline pushing through her veins as they sprint down the hillside. The C-pack on Joule's back clanks with every step. She tightens the shoulder straps of the old banged-up water tank, pretty thrilled that it worked. Up 'til the moment she opened the nozzle, she wasn't sure if she'd followed all the instructions from the YouTube video correctly. But apparently, she'd done a good enough job getting it cleaned it up and working.

It's almost worth all the trouble it made for her—considering *that* was the YouTube video that ended up getting her location traced and run out of her hideout that morning.

There's no time to dwell on her victory. Not while the undead continue to multiply around her, pouring out of the shadows.

These zombies move unlike any of those she's seen before. They're more like a team. More like humans. Except . . . there's no humanity in those terrible faces.

Joule feels a kind of horrible wonder.

There is something very strange going on.

And then the sound of moaning drowns out her thoughts.

It's a day for impossible things here in Redwood, and this is only the beginning.

———————

As the girls run, Nix rages at losing his prize, and regroups with the others. He sees that the main body of the horde has begun to emerge from underground and gather on the battlefield. The tunnel through which he traveled from the mine is minuscule compared to the wide-open mouth of the main tunnel into Redwood, now surrounded by furiously feeding zombies.

Nix shepherds them forward, allowing them to feed, devouring anything in their path—wood, bone, even steel. That terrible hunger that pushes them onward only grows and grows as they get more and more powerful. They quickly catch up to the other, slightly weaker zombies that arrived with Nix over the last few days, and then overtake them—

None of the zombies much care what direction they're going, as long as there's fuel there for the furnaces inside them. This unquenchable need is the lens through which all zombies see the world.

Except for Nix.

What drives Nix out into the world is a different kind of need. A hollowness that isn't easy to name. It's a sore subject. A gut-wrenching question. A loneliness that's all-encompassing.

Right now Nix's attention is fixed on the girls who are running away, scrabbling up the switchbacking trail leading up the steep north side of the valley. One of the girls in particular.

Just as Nix can feel how many other zombies are around by the intensity of the air temperature, he can tell: She's like him. Neither fully human nor fully undead. He's been watching her, and waiting to introduce himself for some time.

It has not gone according to plan, but he's far from defeated.

———————————

As Regina's lungs strain and her legs pump, moving up the little road that zigzags from the bottom of the valley to the ridge above—

"Not that way!" Regina hears the girl with the wild hair call out from behind her. Regina stops, looking back.

"Go with the flow," she says to Regina.

"What?" Regina manages to say.

"It's what my dad always told me. When it's zombie season, and you don't know for sure which direction to go, you just look for signs of water and *go with the flow*. And right now, the flow is there," the girl says, pointing to a rapidly moving brook. "We follow it, take it down to the river, and swim across. You can swim, right?"

"Don't have to swim," says Regina, her throat tight and sore. "That's where I'm going."

She points up toward a big house perched on the edge of the cliff above.

"Is that your *house*?" the girl asks.

Regina doesn't answer.

"Is that—does your house have a *waterfall*?"

It does indeed have a waterfall, among other things.

Like zombieproofing.

In the distance, Regina hears a distant cry for help. Twin cries, actually.

"Darlene and Chanda," says Regina's new companion, panic in her voice. "My friends are in trouble."

14

FLASHPOINT

Oliver searches the shadows, uncertain which way to run. Everywhere he looks, there's a pair of orange eyes, a gust of superheated, rotten-smelling air. Two figures become four, become five, seven . . . eight? No: seven. One after the other, zombies emerge from the giant cave that has just opened, like some kind of portal to another world. They press forward, hands clawing and feet heavy.

It's becoming hard to keep track of all the moaning, hungry, dirty silhouettes. And that's bad news, Oliver knows.

But there's worse news, too, it seems.

Oliver blinks to try and clear his spark-filled vision and make sure he's not hallucinating. No matter how hard he tries to argue with what he's seeing, it's still there. These zombies move unlike any horde he's seen before. They're forming squads, moving in organized teams. Tearing up trees. Flushing out birds and rodents and driving them toward other zombies that simply wait for their food to come to them. And their numbers are still swelling with new zombies climbing from the cave.

Oliver's heart thuds with panic in his chest.

8

8

This feels like the zombie season to end all zombie seasons.

It feels like it's their world now. One humans can't survive.

We need to go, Oliver wants to scream at the girls. But there's a suffocating feeling inside his lungs, and there's no way he can speak.

Oliver reaches down, grabs a rock, and throws it in Darlene and Chanda's direction. It skitters across the ground past their feet, startling them, making them look toward him. He points with a finger to each of them in turn, and then points south, toward the river.

Almost instantly, Darlene and Chanda understand what Oliver is trying to communicate with his frantic gestures. But in the time it takes for them to start moving, the zombies close ranks.

They've seen us, Oliver thinks in terror.

"Ollie!" a girl's voice hisses.

Oliver spins and sees the person he least expects to be there.

Joule Artis.

Chanda and Darlene recognize the voice of their friend and also spin around, their faces full of surprise and joy.

But the joy is very, very short-lived.

Their shouts have drawn interest from the fast-growing horde.

Oliver makes a split-second decision and starts clapping his hands loudly, pulling all the zombies' attention to him. Then he swivels to Joule, hoping she sees what he's doing: distracting the zombies to give the other girls a head start.

But even Joule seems mystified.

It's not until another girl steps forward that Oliver realizes Joule is with someone else. Someone who understands that Oliver is giving them a chance to escape. Luring the monsters away.

With a rush of adrenaline, Oliver leads the zombies on a chase, just like during Manhunt.

If only he had a bag of trash to use as zombie bait right now.

But the zombies stay on his heels.

The heat is intensifying, like being under the brightest sun without any sunscreen. And it isn't just the exposed skin on his face and his arms that's getting burned. No, every time he is forced to inhale, the air is impossible to breathe. His scalded lungs are working as hard as they can, simply to keep him from passing out.

And more zombies, well past counting, are surely inbound by now.

Looking around him, Oliver sees that all his escape routes are now clogged with zombies.

But the brigade is on the way, Oliver reminds himself, suddenly very glad that Chanda didn't listen to him and called for help.

The zombies are now between him and the other kids.

He seems to have the zombies' full attention.

He hopes he has their full attention.

That way, the others might be able to make it out alive.

He heads to the trunk of the sturdiest tree around and grabs hold of a low limb. He heaves himself up onto it and starts to climb as fast as he can.

The zombies grasp the branches below him.

Not climbing. Consuming.

Tearing the tree from its roots.

It's all he can do to keep himself in the tree and keep going higher.

The tree has all it can handle keeping its roots in the earth.

From the higher vantage, Oliver can see that Darlene and Chanda are with Joule and the other girl, running for safety.

Oliver gets up to the height of a rooftop, about forty feet, he guesses, before his trembling arms and numb fingers stop him from going any farther. But the air here is cooler, he discovers. And . . . he can almost breathe like normal again. The sparks start to fade from his vision, and his lungs greedily suck down breath after breath.

He knows there's a team of brigadiers with C-packs on their backs coming at top speed.

He just has to hold out until they get here.

Their heat-sensing infrared goggles had to have spotted this flashpoint from a mile away. But when it's all hot, like it is here, the goggles make everything look the same.

By the time they find him, it might be too late.

Oliver knows that if he can signal the zombiefighters somehow, it'll mean they get here faster. And now that he can breathe again, that means there's nothing stopping him from screaming to let the zombie brigade know where they are.

"BRIGADIERS!" he cries out.

Below, the zombies start to violently shake the tree. It takes all Oliver's strength to hold on.

He can only hope that the zombie brigade has been able to spot his location to within earshot.

"HELLLP! OVER HERE!" he continues to shout, clinging to the trunk of the shivering, groaning tree.

The moans below him drown him out.

The trunk starts to screech and pop as the zombies' fury intensifies.

The zombies want to feed.

15

DECISION

DUSK ALERT: Emergency alert level orange is now in effect throughout Marin County, Sonoma County, Lake County, and Mendocino County. Always remember! Throughout Dusk, flashpoints may arise without warning.

Joule wonders if her father had to make a choice like this.

She sees Oliver in the tree. She sees that it's only a matter of time before the zombies pull the tree down.

She knows she needs to save him.

But . . . there's also Darlene and Chanda and the other girl.

Oliver's distraction is working. This is their one chance to get away.

If they try to save Oliver, the zombies will only turn on them.

The girls will be outnumbered. Overwhelmed. Vulnerable.

"Come on!" yells Joule's new friend. The girl with the zombieproof house at the top of the bluff.

Darlene and Chanda are just as paralyzed as Joule is.

How do I decide? she wonders.

Four of us. One of him.

But still.

That's when Joule sees the zombie brigade heading straight toward the tree.

They've seen Oliver.

Or maybe they've only seen the zombies.

"Look in the tree!" Joule screams.

She's not sure the brigade hears her.

But one of the zombies does. She sees it turn away from the horde.

Toward them.

Four of us. One of him.

What has she done?

Now Darlene is pulling on her arm. "We have to go," she says. "There's nothing we can do for him."

Not deciding has become the decision.

She wonders if her dad did that, too.

Or maybe someone else made that decision about him, and this is how he—

Darlene's voice is more severe now, her pull stronger. "Whatever you're thinking right now, stop it. We've got to get inside that house."

Joule gives in.

It feels like survival . . . but at a cost.

"Inside," says Regina, coughing at the effort.

Regina's new companion follows the raspy command, leading the others across the walkway that makes a bridge over a fast-moving brook, which acts kind of like a moat across the front of her house.

The walkway rises as Regina punches a code into the keypad, forming a zombieproof barricade behind the water.

"This is some house," Regina hears one of the girls say.

Regina doesn't answer. She just watches the road behind them, searching it for zombies. Outside the barricade, everything under the streetlights is calm and still. But in the deepest shadows, there are tiny glints—orange eyes or fireflies, it's impossible to discern.

"I'm Chanda, by the way," the girl who just spoke continues.

Introductions are hastily made. It almost feels ridiculous, getting to know one another's names with zombies at the door.

From what Regina can tell, Darlene and Chanda are fine. Shaken, for sure. But fine.

She's not so sure about the girl wearing the superchiller on her back. Joule. She looks like the casualty of two wars: the one outside her and the one inside.

"You need food," Regina tells her. "This way."

She can see the girl arguing with herself, and then giving in. She nods and follows Regina into her kitchen. Once they get there, safe in the inner sanctum of the house, the girl named Chanda touches Joule's arm and Joule pulls her into a silent hug. The one named Darlene joins them. This isn't a time for words, they all agree without even talking about it. There's too much to say.

Regina is outside this. As always, the house is immaculate. Not a thing is out of place, or showing the slightest trace of dust or wear. But somehow she's the one out of place, in this moment.

She checks the security system. Everything is working. The zombies made it as far as the stream, but without the bridge, they won't get any closer. She can see them on the security screens, and it's hard to tell whether they're enraged or indifferent. They start to turn their attention elsewhere.

There's no way to see what's happening below. If the brigade made it. If the boy is still in the tree.

The girls are too busy consoling one another, reuniting, to catch a glance over Regina's shoulder, to see what she sees . . . and what she doesn't see.

She doesn't tell them anything. Being a friend isn't Regina's strength. Solving problems is what she's good at.

Food, Regina tells herself. *Make yourself useful.*

She goes to the refrigerator and freezer, taking out ice cream, cookies, and a few things to make a salad.

Chanda calls 9-6-6 again and talks to the dispatcher in urgent tones, trying to explain where the boy is. Regina can sense her frustration as she says, "It's a tree. I don't know *which* tree." When she hangs up, she doesn't look happy. "She said she'd pass it along to the people on the scene. I think that's all we can do."

For a moment, Joule simply watches Regina set to work. Chanda and Darlene stand awkwardly close by. Then Joule sinks down onto a stool, staring vacantly across the empty home. She looks at the dirt-caked shoes, and the trail they've left across the clean floor behind her.

"Sorry about your floor," she says.

Regina looks up, and is about to tell her it doesn't matter . . . but she's interrupted by the sound of the garage door opening, and several doors slamming, followed by, *"Gina?"* A moment later, Regina's mother bursts into the kitchen with a look of relief as she sees the group of girls looking back, whole and healthy.

"Is everything—?" Mom asks.

"Fine, Mom," croaks Regina. "We're fine."

"Regina, you can't—why didn't you answer your phone when I—?"

Regina feels in her pocket for her phone, but discovers it's gone. Regina's mother sees this, and understands. "It's okay, I just—I got the notification about the barricade alarm going on, and . . . I couldn't . . ."

"Mom, I'm fine." Regina can't quite summon up an offended tone. For once, for the first time she can remember, she's glad to have her mom hovering.

That's when the sirens rise. At first you can feel them in the center of your chest more than hear them. But then they spool up to a one-note, breathless scream that they hold and hold and hold.

Regina's mom scans the unfamiliar faces in her kitchen, including the ragged-looking Joule. "Hi. I'm Dr. Herrera," she says.

Joule focuses, and for a split second Regina fears that Joule remembers the news that the name Herrera was linked to. But she seems friendly enough when she says, "I'm Joule. That's Chanda and Darlene."

"Right. Joule Artis. Your mother's got quite the flyer campaign going around the city."

Joule blinks and looks away from Dr. Herrera.

Regina looks at Joule, and puts two things together: "You're the one who ran away from home!" she says. "Like, a week ago."

"Three days," says Joule. "Honestly, my mom is a big-time overreactor."

Dr. Herrera doesn't appear to agree. Chanda and Darlene just look very relieved.

"You can take off the tank, if you want," Regina suggests to Joule.

It's clear that Joule forgot she still had the chiller tank strapped to her back. She peels it off and lets it fall heavily to the ground.

"Where'd you even get one like that?" says Regina. "It's ancient."

"I repaired it," says Joule.

Regina looks at her, impressed. "You know how to fix stuff like that?"

"I know how to figure out how to fix stuff."

"That's pretty cool." Regina focuses on preparing the salad. When it's ready, she puts the whole thing in front of Joule, with a hoarse, hesitant, "Thanks . . . for what you did back there."

For the first time, Joule smiles. Weakly, but still, it's there.

Regina's mom checks the security screens again. This time all the girls notice. It's eerily quiet outside, the zombies nowhere to be seen.

"Is everything okay?" Chanda asks.

"Yes," Dr. Herrera says, unconvincingly, as she picks up her cell phone.

"Who are you calling?" Regina asks.

Her mom doesn't answer the question—she just looks around at the other girls' faces. "How many of you girls called your parents and told them where you are?"

Chanda and Darlene look slightly embarrassed and take out their phones. Joule, on the other hand, looks like she's about to be sick.

Dr. Herrera doesn't look surprised by this. "Joule, I'm calling your mother right now. I'm glad these girls helped you, before you got yourself into any *real* trouble . . ."

"Actually?" Regina interrupts. "I didn't help her. She helped me."

"And me," Chanda and Darlene answer together.

"What exactly happened out there tonight, Regina?" Dr. Herrera asks.

"I was out checking on—on something—"

"Alone? At Dusk?" Dr. Herrera gives her a long look. And what surprises Regina the most is her mother's lack of surprise. She hasn't even asked how there came to be zombies outside their door so suddenly.

Regina's mind flashes to the zombieproof coat with the Project Coloma patch and remembers the monster named Nix looming over her.

She wishes her mother would be more surprised.

She turns the puzzle over in her mind as Chanda and Darlene both talk to their parents, and Dr. Herrera offers to take them home. Joule's mother isn't answering, so it's decided that for now, Joule will remain in their house.

Once Dr. Herrera, Chanda, and Darlene have left, Joule and Regina head upstairs. Neither of them has anything to say. Regina helps Joule get set up in the extra bedroom, with sheets and a pillow, and pajamas. But Joule just sits on the unmade bed in her dirty jeans. They sit there, mostly silent, checking for news of Oliver, but instead seeing news about other outbreaks in nearby parts of the state. About a half hour later, Dr. Herrera comes in with Mrs. Artis.

Regina can see Joule is on the edge of tears.

"What can I do?" Regina asks.

"Stay," says Joule. "Please."

Stay. Please. Regina is instantly transported back to the woods, where a zombie calling itself by the name Nix asked her the same thing.

Regina feels hot panic but keeps her cool and nods. "Okay, Joule."

And that's when Mrs. Artis says, "Joule. We need to talk."

Joule looks absolutely hopeless, unable to reply.

16

HOP LIKE HOPE

As the sirens rise, Oliver's friend Del slowly turns around in a full circle, listening to which direction the sound is coming from. Checking his blind spots. All the usual safety measures.

It's hard to explain how you can tell the distance of a siren, unless you've done it yourself all your life. It's like when you see lightning, and hear thunder, and can tell how far away the storm is, and if you listen long enough you can tell if it's getting closer, or farther away . . .

These sirens are very, very close.

As this is happening, Coach is doing a head count. The kids from the neighborhood are all checking in.

"Oliver?" Del calls out.

"We're missing Oliver, Chanda, and Darlene," Coach tells him, expression grave.

"Should we wait?" Del asks.

Coach shakes his head, then calls out, "Usual drill, everyone! Get home, break out the gummy worms, try to get literally one thing done on your homework."

Del knows Coach is right. That he needs to get home now. But that only makes Del more worried for Oliver. He tries calling him, but doesn't get an answer.

What are you up to? Del wonders.

Then something—he's not sure what—makes him shiver.

It's almost like his body knows his friend is in trouble, even if his mind is still asking where he is.

The other kids scatter without a second thought. Just like Del should. Like he's trained to do.

Everyone knows that there will not be any allowances made for missed homework assignments unless the school closes for community-wide zombie-fighting tomorrow. It might sound silly, to worry about homework at a time when zombies are out there, like tonight. But one thing that Del—and all kids who live their lives in the Dusk—learned a long time ago: Some things are too big and complicated for anyone to do anything about. Just focus on dealing with your own kid-sized problems.

Get on with your life. Eat breakfast, go to soccer practice. Do your homework, go to bed. Wake up, have cereal. Take a shower, and don't forget to *"Hop like Hope!"*

"Hop like Hope!" is the slogan from a memorable commercial of a cartoon bunny, Hope the Hare, bouncing into and out of the shower, as quickly as she can. *"Do your part!"* exclaims the cartoon mascot. *"Save water for zombiefighters!"*

It always makes Del cringe-laugh. Like . . . the whole idea of it. If two-minute showers could make zombies go away, we'd all know by now. And going through life dirty and smelly all the time sure doesn't feel awesome. Still, it gets stuck in his head all the time, because it's a really catchy song, and if he stays in the shower past the two-minute egg timer's buzz, he feels like he's as much of a monster as any zombie that's ever walked the earth.

Del sets his guilt aside. He packs it behind a door in the corner of his mind, and focuses all his energy on getting home.

Unlike Oliver, Del is really bad at Manhunt.

He tries to go over the drills in his head . . . but the sirens are getting louder and louder, infiltrating his every thought.

As he gets closer to home, the sirens are so insistent that he realizes:

Something's going wrong. Very wrong.

He's running toward the sirens. Into the danger zone. And as soon as he figures this out, he listens a little closer.

There's another sound that can be heard, underneath the scream of the sirens:

". . . help!"

Del knows whose voice it is.

"Ollie?!" he cries out, turning toward the sound.

Del hears the voice again, and this time it seems to be coming from the other direction.

". . . brigadiers, over here!"

He spins around, his heart pounding.

"OLIVER?" he bellows.

He ignores the screaming sirens and heads toward where he last heard his friend's voice.

———————

Oliver clings to the branch with all his might as the zombies push and pull on the tree, making it creak and groan, like it's in the middle of a huge storm.

The brigade better get here soon, Oliver thinks, calling out again and again. His voice is weaker and weaker. But he has to keep trying.

"Help! Any—*oaaaaa!*" Suddenly, he feels like he's in a roller-coaster cart cresting the hill. The bottom drops out from under him, and he and the tree he's holding on to are both beginning to gain speed downward.

"Ahhh!" he cries out, tumbling to the earth.

Something sharp rakes his skin, drawing blood. It's not clear whether it's a whipping branch or a zombie's nails, and he's too busy trying to figure out if the trunk of the tree that's tumbling with him is about to land on his head to really notice anyway.

He hits the ground hard, all the air forced out of him, and he tries to roll out of the path of the enormous crushing trunk, but there's no time.

With an earthshaking crash, the whole tree lands on Oliver.

Or. It would have, if the trunk hadn't slammed into its neighbor, halting its fall directly over Oliver's head.

Oliver manages a hoarse laugh at his extreme swings of luck.

But in his throat there's a thick sob building.

That's when he sees the zombies, moving closer and closer. Ignoring everything in their path as they lock their eyes on his fallen form. There are a lot more now. The heat of all their bodies is once more scorching his lungs. And to cap it off, the tree above him creaks and groans.

But just as Oliver is about to close his eyes in defeat, he sees a sliver of hope. Oliver rolls fast, getting out of the falling tree's way as it crashes to the ground. It lands, right on top of the zombies that were diving toward him. Forming a barricade to block the next wave behind those.

That's actually really funny, Oliver thinks. But he doesn't laugh. He spins and *runs*.

———

"Ollie!" Del cries out.

He refuses to consider the possibility that Oliver is beyond help, even as at the exact same time it's absolutely clear that Oliver is beyond *Del's* help. He focuses as much as he can, trying to pinpoint his friend, even as another sound emerges under the sirens—the unearthly cry of the zombies.

Del's phone blinks with an emergency alert. But every time he tries to use it to make a call, it refuses to connect.

Maybe there are too many other people trying to get through to the zombie brigade.

How did it all get so out of control so fast?

———

Oliver crashes through the woods. As fast as he can, through the intense heat on all sides of him . . . from the dark, arms reach, fingers stretch, seeking to latch around his legs and hook around his torso. He weaves through them all. And it's totally bewildering, but that feeling of freedom he got when he was marking trails earlier, running free like that—it's even stronger now.

This unexpected confidence he feels as he runs for his life in the woods with zombies on his heels? It's a thrilling discovery. A moment he'll never forget for the rest of his life.

And as he gets his bearings, he realizes: All the zombies are *gone*. He must be faster than he thought.

He hears nearby voices:

"How'd they all get here so fast? You see that huge barrow hole?"

"Never seen something like that before. Thirty feet wide, and who knows how deep? It looked like a tunnel through the rock."

"But where *are* they all? Something is making my hair stand up."

Oliver turns, looking for the voices' owners.

"It's a sneaky one for sure. No clue how they got past us in the upper ward."

Oliver calls out to them. "Brigadiers?! Hello?!"

The conversation suddenly stops. "Who's out there?"

Oliver waves his arms, and calls out, "My name's Ollie! I need some help."

"Ollie!!" he hears a familiar voice call out.

His aunt emerges and crashes into him in a huge hug that melts something inside his heart, and he feels a huge surge of feelings: good ones, bad ones, and unnameable ones, all at once.

"All accounted for, then?" Chief Wachs says to the other zombiefighters once she releases Oliver.

"Aunt C, I have to tell you something," says Oliver. "There's something weird going on out there tonight."

"I have to talk to you as well, Oliver," Chief Wachs says, with a grim seriousness. "But now is not the time."

"You don't understand!" Oliver insists. "The zombies are acting different, and I think—"

She puts up a hand to silence him. "Not now, Ollie. I need to finish my job here. We'll talk later. Rob? Take him home, no detours."

With that, she turns her back on Oliver.

To Oliver's shock, he's bundled away and taken back to a van on the street next to the park. The zombiefighter who's driving him, Rob, doesn't offer up answers to any of Oliver's questions, or listen to Oliver's warnings about the zombies' strange teamwork. He's not just some annoying kid vying for attention—he has real, important information for the zombiefighters.

Oliver feels a buzzing in his pocket and takes out a ringing phone. The one he found on the ground.

The name that comes up is "Regina Computer."

"Hello?" he says, answering the call.

"Hey!" a girl's voice says. "You found my phone."

Her voice is crackling, like the call is breaking up.

Oliver's mind works fast, realizing that this must be the girl he saw with Joule earlier. "You're alive?" Oliver says. "You're all safe?"

The call could get dropped at any moment, but in short order Oliver learns that all is as well as can be hoped with Regina, Joule, Chanda, and Darlene, and he turns his attention back to the question at the front of his mind. "Regina, you saw the same thing I did out there tonight, right?"

"What do you mean?" says Regina.

"We need to tell everyone that these zombies are different. We need to make them believe us. If the zombiefighters don't realize what's going on this season, people are going to die."

After another pause, Regina's voice emerges from the phone, cold and abrupt. "I didn't see anything weird, Oliver. Your eyes are just playing tricks on you. I gotta go, okay? We'll talk soon."

The line clicks and goes dead.

He only half processes what she just said. He's too numb from everything that happened. From the shock of being chased, having a tree fall on him, and most of all: from being ignored and dismissed by the head of the zombie brigade and also by someone else who saw it with their own eyes.

The rest of the ride home, Oliver goes quiet thinking about what he's going to tell his parents when he gets there.

As the van turns onto the block where Oliver lives, it brakes in the middle of the street, where two other trucks with huge C-tanks on them are already parked.

"Hold on, what's that?" Oliver says, craning to see out the windshield.

But it's absolutely obvious what's happening up there. Zombies are tearing apart a house. Well: not *a* house. It's the Roses' house. And the row of homes behind it are already in shambles.

Meanwhile, both of the trucks parked in the street are aiming powerful streams of superchilled H_2O toward the zombies spilling over from the Roses' house toward Del's house.

"Oh no," says Oliver.

But that's not all.

Eventually, Oliver's eyes are drawn to the place he's lived his entire life. And it takes him a long time to recognize, because the roof has been torn apart, and through what's left of the windows, he gets a series of snapshots, like he's looking into a portal to another incomprehensible world. Everything he cherishes . . . is broken into pieces and shoved into zombies' mouths.

Mom. Dad. Kirby.

Oliver pushes open the door of the van and lunges for his home . . . only to be stopped by his mother shouting his name. He sees her with the other neighbors gathered on the street. His sister, Kirby, is crouched on the curb with her knees folded up against her chest. His dad stands a little bit away from everyone else, staring out in shock.

"Ollie. You scared me." His mother checks him head to toe for zombie bites, while Oliver's escort, Rob, fills his mother in on where he was found.

The relief in her eyes is as deep as the ocean. As she wraps him in her arms, he can feel her shaking. Her whole body.

"Okay, Mom," he says. "You wanna hear the story? Or you wanna squeeze me to death?"

She laughs in relief. "I can do two things at once, Ollie," she says. "Three, actually." She pulls him toward where their family car is idling up the street, packed with their go bags and who knows what else.

"It's time to get out of here," she says, releasing him reluctantly. "You get your sister, and I'll get your dad."

"But what about . . . what about the house?"

"It's not important, Ollie. We've gotta go."

Oliver just stares at her, the house, everything.

He goes over to Kirby and offers his hand. She takes it, and he hoists her up.

"You okay?" he asks.

"Am I allowed to say no?"

"Now's the moment you're going to start asking permission?" says Oliver, with a hint of exasperation.

"Where were you?"

"Up a tree. I'll tell you later. Mom says it's time to go."

As they drive away, Oliver catches a glimpse in the window of his bedroom. He thinks about all the maps. The shoebox full of notebooks. Irreplaceable.

Gone.

And then they turn the corner, and the house falls out of view.

Oliver sits there, numb.

His whole world—everything he put such care and energy into. It's all just . . . a meal for the zombies now.

———————

This isn't how Del expected to find Oliver. But there's no doubt in his mind—that's his family's van speeding down the street. Del's breath comes in heaves and gasps as tries to call out to them. He stretches out his arms and waves, but they don't notice. In the dark, maybe they can't tell the difference between Del and a zombie.

The car turns the corner and heads out of sight, and Del keeps running, even though he knows he missed them.

Except then he makes it around the corner. And the car is stopped in the middle of the street.

The van door opens, and Oliver looks out, shocked to see him.

"Del?!"

17

WHY

Regina tries to give Joule and Mrs. Artis privacy as they talk in the spare bedroom, but her brain is in overdrive, making it impossible to sit still. Like a goldfish in a fishbowl that's way too small, her thoughts and memories move back and forth from one to the other as she paces around her room—

The heat is too much for her skin, like a sunburn taking hold. Eyes wide, she sees the terrible hunger of the zombie, powerless to escape. Its jaw hangs open horribly, its eyes blank and chilling. Its hand advances—

All those dirty, sooty fingers curling, reaching—

Regina feels a flash of revulsion as the memory flares in her mind. She tries to push it away, but that only gets her tangled up in it even more.

Stay, Nix says. Please. *His fingers thrust out wide. She feels her mouth grow less and less cooperative. Less and less—in her control. It comes out as a mumble. As . . . a throaty, raw sound.* Your home is with us now.

He watches her, with a horrible, awful, patient smile, as the truth of this statement seems to get more and more undeniable—

Regina pushes back against this with all her willpower. And here in her home, it's easier to dismiss the monster's claim on her, however undeniable it seemed to be while it was happening.

She tests her voice, clearing her throat easily.

She stares at her hands and rubs feeling back into her fingers.

As she heads down the hall to the bathroom to splash water on her face, she sees Joule and her mother through the cracked-open spare bedroom door, sitting on the bed. Messy and full of feelings. Smelly and exhausted and an inch from tears. Regina looks at them together, and starts to get choked up in a way that she never, ever does.

"Psst," Joule whispers.

Regina's eyes shift, meeting Joule's gaze.

"Hey," Joule whispers. "Is my mom asleep?"

Seeing Mrs. Artis's eyes are closed, her arm draped around her daughter, Regina nods.

"Your mom's pretty upset," says Regina quietly.

"She's always like this," Joule says with a sigh. "It's so exhausting sometimes."

"Is that why you left?"

"*She's* the one who's leaving. Not me."

"Oh," says Regina, on awkward and unfamiliar ground with the emotion in Joule's voice. Logic problems that need solving are Regina's native language—but feelings get ooky quickly for her.

"Look, it's kind of a long story," says Joule. "Can we just have a deal where we don't talk about the way we got here, and just focus on what we're gonna do next?"

Regina feels herself grin. "Deal," she says, and they shake hands on it. Very businesslike and proper. "So: What do we do next?"

With the stealth of a bank robber, Joule slips free from her mother, and tiptoes out the door, into the hall. Mrs. Artis apparently didn't sleep for a minute during the whole three days that her daughter was absent, based on how deeply she slumbers now.

Joule nods for Regina to lead, and Regina heads to her bedroom, where she wishes she could just crawl into bed. But as she turns to Joule and is about to say they should call it a night, Joule throws her arms around Regina in a huge hug.

"You're a good friend, Regina," Joule says.

And just like that, the business arrangement has once more fallen apart. The ookyness is back and even more ooky. And yet? Something about Joule insisting that Regina isn't just her friend—but that Regina is a "good" friend . . . ?

It makes Regina want to earn the title Joule has just entrusted to her.

"What's your plan, friend?" Regina asks, stumbling slightly as her mouth forms the word "friend."

Joule runs a hand through her wild hair, and after a moment her head falls with a shrug. This is the moment when a human being would comfort another human being, Regina knows.

You belong with us, her memory taunts her, and it makes a chill go through her chest.

"Right," says Joule. "Okay. It's my dad. You asked before why I ran away? *He's* why. Missing, presumed dead, they say. And my mom, she just . . . So, she says we're moving to New York, like—now. Like—she's so fixated. She booked us a flight for as soon as the curfew is lifted in the morning. Eleven thirty-five out of SFO."

Regina nods. "And you think that your dad . . ."

"I know," says Joule. "Look, I'm not—I know that he's probably—he's probably . . ."

"I get it," Regina croaks.

"I know how I sound. My mom, my friends, all of them think I'm nuts. And that's probably fair, but . . . he needs help. He needs me. I'm a hundred thousand million percent sure of it."

The determination reminds Regina of herself.

"I want to help you, Joule," Regina says.

"Why?" Joule asks.

"I owe you."

Joule shakes her head. "I did you a favor, you'll do the same for someone else one day. That's how it oughta work—not 'owing.'"

Regina frowns. "There's another reason." But as she reaches for the words, her throat's gone all sandpapery and rough again. Regina clears her throat, and starts talking, before she loses her nerve.

"You don't know me really well, but I . . . I want to be a good friend for you." Regina's voice cracks, and she says the rest in a hurry. "Everyone at school thinks I'm weird and too intense because I get more excited about the work my parents do than, like, whatever video is trending. Not that there's anything wrong with that stuff! I just, I don't know, I kinda get the sense that maybe you understand where I'm coming from?"

Joule nods slowly. "I get it. I mean, my friends are great—they braved a zombie horde to find me! But sometimes I feel like there are two Joules: the person I act like around other people to make them happy, and the weirdo who hides out in a barn and gets way too close to zombies." Joule smiles. "I guess you and I can be weirdos together."

Regina fills with embarrassment and gratitude. "Are you sure? I'm just some girl you met an hour ago."

"Just some girl? Come on. I know the stuff your parents do for a living. Your family works for HumaniTeam! Solving the zombie problem!"

"When did you put that all together?"

"I pay attention to things!"

"And you still want to be my friend?"

"Of course. I know none of that was *your* fault."

Regina shifts uncomfortably. "It's . . . complicated."

"Yeah, everything feels complicated these days. And I used to *like* complicated. You should see these dishes I used to make with my dad. The more steps, the better. I even made Baked Alaska a few times! You know, the ice cream cake you make in the oven?"

Regina looks impressed. "You made Baked Alaska? It's like the most delicious science experiment. Baking is basically chemistry."

"Yes!" Joule says with a laugh. "I knew we had stuff in common. Maybe I can turn in a soufflé instead of my science homework."

"It probably depends on what type of science class. I'm in Earth Science this year so I'm not sure it'd be exactly right, but—"

Joule cuts her off with an embarrassed laugh. "Sorry, that was supposed to be a joke."

Regina blinks. "Oh."

"We'll workshop it," says Joule.

"Sorry?"

"That's what me and Dad always say, when one of us tells a bad joke."

Regina nods. "We'll workshop it," she says.

Joule's smile shines through on her face again.

"You really believe in him," says Regina.

"Other way around. *He* really believes in *me*."

"Right."

"So, y'know . . . how can I give up?"

"You can't," Regina says with a determination that turns Joule's head.

"And yet. I'm leaving for New York in the morning. And my mom isn't likely to let me to be out of her sight until we're strapped into our seat belts and the cabin door is closed." Joule seems to deflate.

Regina pokes at the problem in her mind, thinking. But Joule distracts her, inhaling sharply.

"What's wrong?" Regina follows Joule's gaze—

Outside, in the tree that looks in on her window, two orange eyes stare, not blinking at all.

Even though it's dark, and even though the zombie is on the other side of the wall, Regina knows it isn't just any zombie.

It's Nix.

She can barely make out his expression, but there's a need in his burning eyes.

He crooks a finger, making a clear gesture.

COME.

Before Regina can react, Joule grabs the glass of water from the bedside table, like it could possibly quench the zombie's furnace-like heat, and moves between Regina and the zombie outside the window.

But at the sight of Joule he's gone, the night's darkness complete once more.

Joule looks at Regina in utter confusion. "Did you just—what was—did you just *see that?*"

Just like before, Regina finds her throat too tight to speak.

"Regina?"

"Yeah," Regina croaks, relieved to get a word out.

Joule looks down at Regina's hands. "You're shaking," she says.

When Regina looks down, she sees a tremor is going through her fingers. She makes her hand a flat blade and brings it down against her palm: *stop.*

"I'm fine." Regina wiggles her fingers to prove it.

Joule keeps an eye on Regina, but her eyes flit to the window as well.

"Um, Regina? This is an awkward question, but . . ."

"Why are zombies, like, weirdly fixated on me?" Regina asks.

"Uh-huh. Also, was that the same zombie as earlier? Is it hunting you or something? Did it just climb into view of your bedroom window in the middle of the night to see you?"

"I don't know, I don't know—"

"Sorry," says Joule. "Meant it as a joke."

"Hey. Wanna hear something completely unbelievable?"

Joule looks at her, attentive.

Regina swallows hard. She knows if she hesitates, she'll never be able to go on. "I—so when you found me today? That zombie—he talked to me? And . . . told me I belonged with them. Told me I *was one of them*. And when he said that—"

Regina falters, feeling her throat getting stiff again.

Very gently, Joule says, "Regina, I was there. It didn't say anything. Zombies can't talk."

"I know they can't talk. But this one did. And I'm afraid it might . . . I'm afraid I might be . . ."

Regina lifts her gaze to Joule's face, the horror clear. She falls silent, unable to finish the sentence.

Joule wraps her arms around Regina in a tight squeeze. "Okay, anyone who is feeling as much as you're feeling right now is like the total opposite of a zombie. I promise."

As Joule releases Regina and meets her gaze, Regina can feel Joule's conviction enveloping her like an embrace. Naming a terrible fear out loud to a friend is an antidote to its power.

And as she and Joule say good night a little while later, with her new friend insisting on sleeping in a pile of blankets on the floor, Regina starts to feel more like herself than she has in a very, very, very long time.

———————

From a distant hiding place, Nix continues to watch the story unfolding inside the Herreras' home. It's like a play on a stage, only he can't remember ever having seen a play, and doesn't remember what a stage is, either.

He knows there is far too much work to do for him to make friends right now. If that's indeed what he wants. Nix isn't sure why he is drawn to this human. Maybe to be with her. Maybe to destroy her.

He turns away from Regina's window and strides back onto the battlefield, ready to lead his multiplying horde.

18

"Thanks, Mrs. Wachs," says Del, out of breath from running.

"Move over, Kirby," Oliver tells his sister as Del slams the door of the minivan. Or: he tries to slam it. The extra-slow electric motor makes a whizzing sound of protest and takes over, pulling the door slowly, *slowly* closed.

If there'd been any zombies chasing after Del, that would've been the end of the movie. Cut to black, roll the credits.

But they get lucky this time, and the door latches shut.

Del buckles his seat belt. "Heard you shouting," he tells Oliver.

"Got chased up a tree!" Oliver says excitedly.

"Wow."

"Yeah. Then the tree fell on me!" Oliver adds.

Del looks at Oliver with dismay. "Wow."

"Don't worry, I'm fine," Oliver says. "It was actually awesome. Except for the whole almost-being-eaten part."

Del frowns, not saying anything.

Oliver's mother looks at Del in the rearview mirror. "How are you, Del? Are you hurt?"

"I'm fine. I saw our houses," Del says with a nervous tone.

"I know, it's unbelievable," Oliver says. "They're totally gone. Everything."

"Are my mom and dad—?"

Oliver's mom keeps focused on Del as she drives. "Your parents went out looking for you and the rest of the other kids."

"My phone isn't connecting," Del says. "Can you try and call them?"

"The cell tower is overloaded here. We should have better luck when we get a little farther from the flashpoint."

"Oh," Del says. "Okay."

"I don't know why we're leaving, though," Oliver says. "We should hang around and help the brigadiers."

No one responds to him for a minute.

"I said, maybe we should hang around and—"

"We all heard you, buddy," Oliver's mom interrupts him.

"Well, is anybody gonna answer me?"

"We're going to the zomb shelter at the high school, Oliver. Del, that's where your folks will head to as well, even if the phones are out of commission."

"Thanks, Mrs. Wachs," Del says thinly.

The rest of the way to the high school, they all ride in silence. A couple times, Oliver looks over at Del, and Del has this weird look on his face. It's a look like . . . like you know when there's a zombie coming toward you, and it's just eating rocks right now, but you're keeping an eye on it anyway? Never turning your back, in case it sneaks up and jumps out in your face?

Exactly. It's that kind of look.

As Oliver starts to feel a ramping anger at what's going on around him, Oliver's mother parks the car in the lot in front of the high school, which is bustling with activity. It's been converted into a zomb shelter tonight. Bristling with defenders on the roof and packed full of zombie counter-measures, zomb shelters are designed to save human life by convincing zombies to move on and find an easier meal somewhere else.

It's also where the mobile command post for the zombie brigade had been set up, in this case. A dozen different emergency vehicles are lined up one after the next: freeze engines, purifying tankers, everything.

Oliver eyes it, and his mom sees him eyeing it.

"Don't even think about it, Ollie."

"Mrs. Wachs?" Del interrupts. "I'm gonna go in."

"We're right behind you," she replies.

At her nod, Del half hurries, half drags his feet into the zomb shelter, looking for his parents. Oliver's dad and sister follow.

"Wait a sec, Mom. I just want to see if Aunt Carrie is back," Oliver says, trying to sound calm and reasonable.

She firmly points him toward the gymnasium doors.

"Absolutely not, buddy. If your aunt is distracted dealing with you, that means that whatever she's *supposed* to be doing isn't getting done. Do you understand?"

"But—"

"No. This isn't a time when we negotiate, Oliver. Carrie is out there saving lives and stopping zombies, and she—"

"—And she could probably use all the help she can get with that." A surge of frustration bubbles up inside Oliver. How could anyone argue with him trying to help in an emergency, when people need all the help they can get?

"Buddy, please don't do this," says his mother, with a warning tone.

Oliver is stunned. "What did *I* do?"

"You still want to do your C-pack certification with the rest of your classmates in the fall? This is a good time to prove to me that you're patient enough to handle that responsibility."

Oliver looks at her, mouth hanging open at her totally uncalled-for threat. "Mom, you have to be kidding. The zombies are *here*, and everything we own is *gone*, and you're talking about being patient? Taking a class? *In the fall?* I don't know if you've noticed it, but the world is ending right *now!*"

"Well, kiddo, you just lost the parent's signature you need for that permission slip."

"Uggggh!" Oliver screams. "I cannot believe the weird things you choose to care about."

"World's been ending for a long, long time, Oliver. What you're doing right now? Not helpful."

"Don't I know it," he mutters to himself, eyeing the zombie brigade vehicles lined up across the parking lot. "And what are *you* doing about it?"

She smiles sadly. "I ask myself that a lot, kiddo," she says as they head into the gymnasium, where the sound of a crying baby drowns out everything else.

On the other side of the parking lot, at the mobile command post that the zombie brigade has set up, there's a weariness and a discontented feeling among the zombiefighters who pass by one another as they move from one emergency to the next.

"You see our canal did zilch to slow 'em down?"

"All the work we did to get it dug over the winter . . ."

"And the bait we dumped in their path?"

"Couple years ago we'd bait a trap half that good and snare dozens."

"Hundreds."

"Stop a flashpoint in one go. These ones?"

"Barely even sniff it."

"That's enough chatter, folks," says a woman in a stiff, zombieproof coat as she crosses from the mobile command post to her waiting cruiser.

"Yes, Chief!"

Chief Wachs continues at a rapid pace. "Come on, I know it's early in the season still, but let's get our act together, huh?"

There's still a cautious quiet throughout much of Redwood. No panic. Not yet. Even though the sirens continue to scream and the emergency alerts have erupted from every phone in the county.

Those sort of warnings are normal during zombie season. Folks have been through them enough times to get used to the feeling, and not "overreact" to every little flashpoint that the zombie brigade quietly and routinely squashes.

But Chief Wachs is worried. For as many zombie reports as have come in to 9-6-6 tonight, the zombies have proven hard to pin down. When her freeze trucks rush in, hoses open wide, the zombies barely put up a fight. But then? Another call comes in: A different flashpoint has popped up nearby. It's very peculiar. And all the while, thermal images say that it's a hot zone on the whole north side. So hot that her instruments are basically useless.

It's going to be a very long night.

19

NIGHTMARE VS. REALITY

Nix has been away too long.

During his absence, the others have gotten distracted and spread out too much, leaving themselves vulnerable to the zombiefighters, who are throwing all the water they can find at the horde. Nix can feel the other zombies' weakened state in the way the heat around him is starting to ebb.

It's time to get back to command.

Time to focus.

He needs to bring all the different groups of zombies moving through this city together, like fingers coming together to make a fist.

———

Del has not found his parents in the zomb shelter at the high school, and he's taken up watch outside on the curb, staring at all the people coming and going. His phone battery is running low. No signal, no word—but still he has to check every minute, just to be sure.

Oliver sits with him, and tries to ignore the zombiefighters doing all the things he's not allowed to do. He tries to distract Del from his worries about why his parents aren't back, but it isn't easy. Oliver can't help but imagine them running for their lives, getting stuck in a tree. Like he did. With zombies shaking it, tearing its roots from the earth. He imagines the tree falling, the steel-strong arms grasping for them, the throat, the ankles—

This should be the moment Oliver shows up with a C-pack and soaks the zombies, saving the day.

He can do it. He knows he can do it.

Oliver silently makes a bargain with the universe—he'll do whatever it takes to get the chance to make a difference like that.

As Oliver returns to reality, he notices Del is fixated on his phone again.

It reminds him of the phone he found earlier that evening, and he recounts the story to Del. How he found the clue that led to finding Joule Artis, met up with her and Regina . . .

"Regina? As in Regina Herrera?" Del interrupts, handing the mystery phone back to Oliver. "As in, the girl whose parents were involved in that super weird project up in the mountains?"

Oliver nods, and looks out across the parking lot at the brigadiers moving around the command post. He thinks about how Regina refused to believe that the zombies were able to follow orders, work as a team. "Del, did you see anything weird about the zombies out there tonight?"

"Huh?" says Del. "Like what?"

Oliver sees Del staring around, not really paying attention. Del has his own things to worry about, it's clear. "Don't worry about it, Del," says Oliver.

"Sorry," says Del. "I'm spaced out."

"It's okay," says Oliver.

"You really wanna go back out there again tonight, Ollie?"

"I wanna be helping right now, not hiding."

Oliver keeps watching the brigadiers.

Del's shoulders sink and he looks at the ground.

"I wanna help, too," he says uncertainly.

———

Among the zombies, Nix can feel the sting of the freeze trucks' supercooled water the same way he feels the heat of the horde. It's enraging to lose his forces like this.

Once they're tightly packed together, there'll be no amount of supercooled water that will be able stop them. Until then, Nix moves swiftly and stealthily. Keeping tabs on the zombiefighters, directing each separate group of zombies to retreat at the moment a freeze truck arrives, and feed somewhere else. It's simple for Nix to keep the brigade running from place to place, wasting their time and their water, while Nix's forces strengthen.

He feels the heat intensify again as he draws his forces together, closer and closer. Even though the zombiefighters keep trying different strategies to destroy the zombies.

What the zombiefighters don't know is that Nix can strategize, too.

———

Chief Wachs crosses the high school parking lot, loosening up the bindings of the zombieproof coat that's tight against her skin. It makes her sweat buckets even as it keeps her safe from the zombies' powerful grasp and the intense heat of the horde.

As she enters the command post, she's hit with a blast of cool air.

It's always a relief, coming out of the fight and being smacked in the face by the power of the superchillers. There's no better zombiefighting tools anywhere in the world. Modern superchillers really are like magic— and yet every six months, the geniuses at HumaniTeam seem to find another breakthrough that makes their chillers twice as powerful against the zombies.

But tonight, all that waterpower has done little more than to slow the really unsettling wave that's moving through Redwood, building strength as it consumes. Somehow, she has gotten steamrolled by a swarm that seems to be able to take anything the brigade throws at it. Tearing through schools and restaurants and homes. It simply rolls over everything.

In the mobile command post of the zombie brigade, the team is studying a video feed from one of her freeze trucks. A clash with the undead. Yes, an entire chunk of the leafy north side of the valley shows damaged homes, fallen trees—but the brigade keeps fighting. The freeze trucks keep spraying hundreds of gallons of supercooled water onto the horde, draining whole swaths of zombies of the energy in their superheated blood. Neutralizing them, so they cannot do any more harm.

"Just focus on dealing with the problem in front of you, Carrie," she reminds herself.

"Chief? Call for you from Celeste Herrera."

Speaking of problems. Chief Wachs feels a heaviness in her chest. Dr. Herrera always used to help the zombie brigade in any way she could. She'd always made sure that the town got the best deal on the best equipment. And if the brigadiers had a question Dr. Herrera didn't know the answer to, she always went hunting for it and found something helpful to share. Dr. Herrera had always been an irreplaceable resource for Chief Wachs in her work.

But then there was Project Coloma. Whatever happened up there in the mountains. She stonewalled every investigation, buried the truth a thousand feet deep. She undid all the good that HumaniTeam built up over years and years with that cover-up.

"I'm not available," she says.

She has more important things to do than talk shop with a scientist who cares more about her work than about all of humanity.

———

In the middle of the night, Regina and Joule startle awake at the sound of the garage door opening. By the time they come downstairs, Mrs. Artis has figured out how to turn on the coffee maker and watches it drip drip drip like sand in an hourglass.

"The most relevant basic unit of time," Mrs. Artis tells the girls as they enter, "isn't a day, or a heartbeat; it's the space of time you have to wait between starting the coffee and drinking the coffee." As the girls look at each other and try to make sense of this, Mrs. Artis pours a cup of coffee and takes a sip, and focuses on Regina. "Your mom went to work," she says.

"Your mom went to *work*?" Joule asks Regina.

Regina just blinks. "I guess so."

Mrs. Artis continues, "She says there's something urgent that came up. But she trusts you to keep the house from getting torn apart until she gets home, Regina."

———

As the horde regains its single-minded, directed purpose, Nix prepares to lead them, down the streets, toward the core of the city.

A freeze truck full of zombiefighters parks itself in their path, aiming its powerful hoses at the horde, spraying hundreds of gallons of pure, super-cooled H_2O that soaks the front rank of zombies.

By now, the brigadiers are beginning to catch up to Nix's strategy. They've grown more aggressive in how they deploy their freeze trucks, expecting the rest of the zombies will retreat.

Not this time.

This time, Nix marshals his forces forward into a tightly gathered, powerful battering ram.

The crew of the freeze truck realizes far too late that they are extremely exposed.

The truck still wipes out the first rank of the zombies, but the second wave of zombies tramples over the extinguished bodies. By the time the rear of the pack moves past the spot where those zombies were destroyed, there's nothing remaining of them on the ground. The undead devour their own just as they would do with any other fuel source they stumble upon.

The horde presses onward. The zombies surge forward and swarm, over-powering the freeze truck, tearing it apart piece by piece.

Nix watches his forces feed and strengthen with satisfaction, even despite his own needs being as yet unfulfilled.

He senses the small contingent of zombies he's left back at the Herreras' house, where his own individual interests lie. Not enough to get inside the heavily fortified compound. But enough to guard. To alert him of any opportunity that might arise.

When Dr. Herrera's car revs its powerful engines and races out of the driveway, they seize the moment and try to climb inside and get into the house.

But as the metal gate rises again, the undead are pushed back out. Their fists leave marks in the metal, but just as they have throughout the night, every time they touch the fence, it steals the heat from their whole arm, as the supercooled water hidden inside the fence does its work on the undead.

A few moments later, the curtains in the upstairs bedroom flutter open and closed, as the girl keeps watching them watching her . . .

Nix waits patiently for the right opportunity.

The march toward the center of the city requires his full focus anyway. To Nix's annoyance, these zombiefighters now better appreciate that they've been underestimating their enemy. They keep what they believe to be a safe distance from the inhuman avalanche bearing down on them.

You're not safe this time, Nix thinks.

He feels no need to warn them of their mistake.

20

THE ZOMB SHELTER

It's an hour before dawn, and the air-conditioning in the gymnasium has already quit in defeat. The thermometer outside is almost a hundred degrees and rising fast. And Oliver lies awake on his cot, sweating, as the sirens and flashing lights bleed through the tall windows above him.

He doesn't even know what's going on out there. The world could be ending, and he's just watching it happen. Not even watching! Every fiber in his body itches to get up. To *act*.

"I gotta get up," he announces, then swings his legs to the ground and pulls his shoes over the socks he never ever took off.

"Ollie?" his dad calls to him from the cot next to his, where Kirby is tucked in beside him, eyes open, totally silent. "It's too early to get up."

Ollie sits there and feels an angry heat growing inside him. He looks down and sees the last remaining beat-up notebook that spent the night under his pillow. Somehow it's fallen on the ground, where it's picked up a coating of gritty, tacky gunk. He wipes at it, getting nowhere.

"Ah, forget it," he says, dropping it back onto the bed.

He already wrecked the thing, trying to copy down from memory all the stuff from the maps and other notebooks that have long since become zombie lunch. None of it came out right, though. Like a copy of a copy. Like a robot reciting a joke.

"Hey, buddy." Oliver's father startles him as he eases down next to him on his cot.

"Dad, come on," he says, scooting away down the bed. He feels that hot anger spreading, and he whispers, "We're just sitting here, while Del's parents are still out there." He looks at where Del's asleep in the next bunk, curled up with his legs to his chest. "Why aren't we out there looking for them?"

"You're a kid, Ollie," says Dad. "You can't join the zombie brigade."

Hearing these words makes him feel helpless, which floods him with shame. "You don't understand."

"I understand just fine, buddy. It's just that—Oliver, this is not a situation where action saves lives. That time has passed. We are living with the consequences of our collective past actions. And there's very little we can do except deal with them. One at a time."

Oliver slumps sideways again, so his torso is flat against the bed, even though his feet are still on the floor.

His dad sits there with him.

Oliver's parents have this ability to pour cold water on everything. Making it all so unclear, uncertain.

"When I was growing up," his dad says, "we never prepared for any of this. Like another lifetime, you know? We'd heard a story or two, maybe, but we never *knew*—how could we have *imagined* it'd be like this?" He gestures at the gymnasium, full of people wrested from their homes. "And all the stuff that I worked so hard to be good at—like, when I think of all the time I spent trying to learn how to throw a curveball? All the stuff I love to do and believe in—it feels . . . It's so hard to make anything feel important in the face of life and death."

Oliver looks at his father, waiting for him to get to the point. But he's done talking, it seems. Now he just stares off, lost again.

"Okay. I gotta go pee," Oliver tells him.

He crosses the wooden, heavily waxed floor, shoes squeaking all the way to the locker rooms.

It's too much, what his parents want from him. His dad wants a redo on his own childhood. And his mom? She sees the world from the point of view of a person reading someone else's story in a book—one of thousands and thousands of books in her library—not a person *living* their story. It's all so easy for them. They don't really care about what happens to the world his generation is stuck with, Oliver decides. Not enough to get out there and make a difference here and now, like Oliver would.

Outside, the sound of the zombie brigade fighting and the horde's moaning and destruction is amplified by the tile walls of the locker room. It feels like the moaning is inside his head, kind of.

It's distracting and exhausting.

All the things he's spent half his life figuring out and organizing and making sense of—all gone, all lost. The world is all unknowns and dangers now. The map has been lost.

Action is what he needs. Actions are what count.

All he has to do is march right across the parking lot to the zombie brigade's command post. That's what he's gonna do.

He leaves the locker room through the door that leads out to the hallway, not back to the gym. And in the silent corridor lit only by emergency lights, he feels like he's got a purpose again. He's a fighter—he knows that now.

Del wouldn't be able to sneak away like this. He wouldn't think to just go up to the brigadiers and volunteer. But Oliver remembers how it felt, when Manhunt went from practice to reality. That's what he's supposed to do with his life. It feels so good to know exactly what all the work's been leading up to, finally.

He gets the whole way to the lobby that leads out to the parking lot without being noticed by anyone. "Just like Manhunt," he mumbles to himself.

He pushes out the door and finds—

The parking lot is empty.

All the brigadiers are *gone.*

"There you are!" his mom says, seeing him standing there, trying to figure out how his plans went wrong.

Oliver turns to her, and sees that she's with his dad, Kirby, and Del.

"What's going on?" he asks.

"Evacuation order just got issued. We have to go."

"*Evacuate?* Mom, Dad—*no.*"

"Come on, Oliver," his father says. "We can't stay here, *but* they got us into a hotel by the beach."

"The *beach?* No."

"You love the beach."

"I'm not going to the beach."

Oliver's mother's eyes trace her son's face. The cheerfulness fades.

"You don't have a choice, Oliver."

"We barely even tried to stop them. How can you just give up?"

Now Mom's mad. "*We* are not giving up. A mile and a half from here, the brigade is putting their lives on the line trying to save the city. But it's *your* job to make sure that they don't have to worry about rescuing *you.* Right now, that means getting in the car and leaving Redwood for a little while. Not forever."

"You don't know how long it'll be before we get to come home," he argues. "Whatever 'home' even means now." For Oliver, the anger's grasp on him is kind of like armor. It shields him, makes all the cold water his mom pours over his ideas just evaporate, unable to get through to where he's vulnerable.

"This isn't the time, buddy." She glares at him in a battle of wills.

"I want to fight, Mom." He's not quite so weak anymore. "Dad?!"

His dad takes her side, of course. "Help your sister out," he says. "We need to get moving."

"Everything's out of control," Oliver tells them. "Do you two even notice that?"

Oliver is too angry to recognize that something about this fight is making his mom look very sad. But Del notices. And Kirby notices.

As Dad goes for the car, Kirby looks toward Del. And Del looks at Oliver.

"Don't be a brat, Oliver," says his soon-to-be-former best friend, on behalf of his soon-to-be-disowned sibling.

That's when the van pulls into the parking lot and right up to the curb.

"Everybody ready to go?" asks Oliver's father.

"Dad—"

"Oliver, not now," his mother interrupts. "We're getting in the van."

As soon as the doors slam shut, an unhappy silence takes hold. And in that moment, their phones all erupt with the same notification:

DUSK ALERT: To support your local zombiefighters in their fight against the fast-moving and explosively powerful Rogue Wave, a mandatory evacuation is ordered for the city of Redwood and surrounding communities. Get to safety! When in doubt, follow the flow!

"That's a little bit late," Del remarks.

"Yeah. Looks like the phones are back, though," says Oliver's dad.

Blood rushes to Del's face as he realizes what this means. With his phone pressed to his ear, he holds his breath and listens as it rings.

21

CLOUDBUSTER

After Regina's mother left at such a strange hour to go to work, Regina sank deep into her thoughts.

What would make Mom leave? What is she working on, in the middle of a zombie invasion?

And what's with Mom rushing home in the first place, when she couldn't reach me on the phone?

She's scared, Regina thinks. And not of something general. She's scared of something specific. And whatever that something is, she can't talk about it.

It's a secret, even now.

It's a secret, even after everything she's shared with Regina.

Is she scared for herself?

That doesn't seem right.

Is she scared for me?

Obviously, she thinks Regina can take care of herself. But she rushed home before anyone knew how bad the Rogue Wave would become.

Does that mean she knew things would get bad tonight? Before anyone else?

Regina has given up waiting for her mother to explain, and she's been digging through all the notes she can find in her parents' home office. Seeking explanations for where the zombies in the NRG came from. For how they could have escaped and made their way to Redwood. For how Nix could possibly exist, and what that means. For HumaniTeam. For humanity. For Regina herself.

Meanwhile, everything with a screen is buzzing with alerts. Mandatory evacuations are in effect—and Dr. Herrera hasn't called. Regina sits at the desk in her parents' home office, the landline phone in her hand. Thinking. It rings three times before her mom answers.

"Honey? What do you need?"

"Hey, Mom. Are you coming home?"

Her mother sounds strained. "Can't right now, Regina. Whatever comes up, I need you to deal with. Okay? Love you—"

"Mom."

Her mother pauses as she's about to hang up the phone. "What is it, Regina?"

Regina closes her eyes. She feels the coolness coming from Dr. Herrera— the demand for logical, concrete answers. And Regina feels an unnameable frustration.

"Why aren't you coming home, Mom? There's an evacuation."

"You'll be safe in our house." Regina's mother barely hesitates, but Regina knows her too well to be fooled.

"Why can't you tell me what's really going on, Mom?"

The silence is longer now. "Honey."

"Why are you scared, Mom?"

Because she is her mother's daughter, Regina knows "Why?" is a powerful question—and the answer will tell you a lot about a person. More than their actions will.

As the silence stretches, Regina is brought right back to the aftermath of Project Coloma. The panic, the fear, the tragic destruction. She feels that choking feeling in her throat, and she fights it back down.

"Does this have anything to do with the generator? With what happened in the mine?"

Talk, Mom, Regina silently pleads.

In her ear, she hears something between a laugh and a sob.

Regina wants to reach through the phone and squeeze her. Never has she felt quite as worried as she suddenly feels in this moment—a gulf threatening to open up under her.

"Mom? Talk to me."

———

"Where are you, Mom?" Dr. Herrera hears, in the midst of a scene of chaos. There are HumaniTechs everywhere, racing around, trying to prepare Project Cloudbuster for launch.

"Regina, I—" Dr. Herrera doesn't know what to say.

She looks around her. A huge weight settles on her shoulders.

She turns her back and starts walking away.

"I'm coming home, Regina," she says. "Sit tight. Don't leave the house. Okay? Whatever anyone else tells you, stay inside, away from windows. Don't let the Artises leave, either."

Behind her, a fleet of rockets are being filled with dry ice. Solid carbon dioxide, at intensely cold temperatures.

It's something that's never been attempted before.

Something dangerous.

22

JAMMED

Del just keeps hitting redial on speakerphone. Every time it rings, everyone in the car feels their nerves jangle, too. Oliver, Kirby, their parents—they all sit in tense silence as it rings and rings. And then, when a voice picks up, their breath catches in their throats.

"Hi, this is Danny, leave a message. Hope you have a great day."

Oliver sees Del's stony, clenched expression as he hangs up and tries again. For the fourth time. *Hope you have a great day.* Oliver sneaks a glance at his best friend, wondering if that might be the last thing Del ever hears his father say.

Oliver looks out the window.

It's the moment of sunrise, when the wind blows strong, and bright light moves quickly across the sky over everything, making it look more like Mars than Earth. It's a haunting moment. Zombie season's grand entrance has arrived, with a full orchestral score . . .

Then there's a beep. Call waiting. Del almost drops the phone.

"Hello?" says Del with barely any sound, somehow both speaking and holding his breath. "Mom?"

"Hi, sweetie." Del's mom's voice emerges from the speaker, thin and far-away. "How are you?"

"I'm fine, I'm with the Wachses."

"Good. Where are you?"

"I'm in their car. We're . . . I don't know. Where are we, Mr. Wachs?"

Out the window, Del can't see much. The Wachs family car is among the dozens of cars that are stuck all waiting to merge into the traffic on the main road, which is also jammed and full of honking cars.

"Hi, Carole." Oliver's dad speaks up. "We're on Fremont, making our way on the north side evacuation route. We can meet up with you—can you send your location?"

"No, don't come to us. We're down near Riverside, and it's—" The phone gets garbled, and everyone holds their breath. ". . . heading toward the river. It's pretty wild."

Oliver can see Del's grip on the phone tighten, and his fingers start to shake. His whole body is shaking, actually. "Mom? Are you still there? What's going on?"

The line has gone dead.

"We have to go get them," Del says. "They said they were heading toward the river."

Oliver's mom reaches out and tries to squeeze Del's hand. "They also told us not to go to them. We have no idea what it's like there. I'm sure they want you to be safe, and the only way to be safe is to get out of here."

Del pulls his hand away from her. "But that's why we have to get them out, too!"

Del unclicks his seat belt and lunges for the door.

Oliver's dad is faster, locking the doors and making it impossible for Del to unlock.

Oliver just watches, feeling detached from the situation. He's pretty sure he could break the window and crawl out, leading Del to the river, to find his parents at just the crucial moment. But then, as Oliver tries to turn this plan into action, his mother snaps, "Oliver, stay out of it! This isn't about you. Not everything is about you."

Oliver freezes, his eyes moving to Del, a silent question in his look.

Del just . . . slumps, looking at the floor. Oliver can see how much it's killing him.

"It's going to be okay, Del," Oliver's mom promises.

"How can you know that?" Del asks.

What's even worse is that it's not like the traffic is moving that fast. The good news is that everyone is evacuating . . . and the bad news is that everyone's evacuating. They're stuck in a long line of cars being sent down both lanes of the one old road on this side of the river that winds its way up to the top of the ridge and out of town. All the way to the Pacific Ocean, eventually. But at this rate it'll take the rest of Oliver's life. A life that seems likely to be shorter and shorter by the minute.

Oliver can do nothing other than watch as they inch along. But as the sun creeps higher into the sky in the rear window, Oliver does get a glimpse of the river below and the bridge crossing over it—he knows that's where the brigadiers are battling the zombies. He thinks of all the people down there. Risking their lives. With Chief Carrie Wachs by their side. He imagines himself there, soaking zombies and saving the day—but instead he's just strapped in, watching the world continue to end.

23

THE BRIDGE

"Focus up. *Everyone*." Chief Wachs looks around her command as the sun rays hitting the dust-laden air bathe the entire landscape in a smoky crimson.

She looks around at her brigadiers, nearly a hundred of them. And five freeze trucks, with all the purifying tankers and other support vehicles. It's nothing to sneeze at, but it's still a small-town organization. Built to keep the peace, not extinguish a full wave.

And in normal circumstances, that would be the end of the story—but this wave is far from normal.

"I understand what I'm asking you to do. Holding a line against something like *that*? It goes against all your instincts. And mine. But these zombies have been testing our assumptions about them all night. This horde seems set on pushing straight through to the center of the city, and we will turn that blind determination against them."

The chief points toward the avalanche of bodies. Thousands upon thousands of incredibly strong zombies tumbling over one another, moving steadily toward the bridge that leads across the wide river separating the leafy, spread-out north side from the dense, working downtown.

"This bridge is the only way for them to cross the river. But if we can take their first punch, folks . . . it's only gonna get easier after that."

If the brigade can hold the bridge, the horde will use up all their energy. They'll weaken and disperse, back to where they came from. That's the theory anyway, and the Regional Director of Emergency agrees: It could work.

But it might be too late already. The wave has doubled in size almost by the hour. Even worse, they've stayed tightly bunched up, not spreading out wide like waves normally do. And if the brigade *can't* stop them, and this Rogue Wave heads on across the river? It'll be like a bomb going off. No amount of zombiefighting will save the city.

Chief Wachs looks up the hillside again.

Her brain has a hard time processing the horror. The zombies surging through the darkness to devour her hometown . . . This isn't something people have words for. The destruction is on a scale too large for a human mind to make sense of.

But everyone here can see what they're up against just as well as she can.

She can see her brigadiers bristling to fight.

"We're gonna focus on the problem in front of us, and we're gonna put our whole heart into it. Clear the streets, hold the bridge, make the city safe."

She scans the faces of the brigadiers around her, one by one. The zombie brigade, mounted up on their freeze trucks and purifier tanks . . . Resolved. Ready.

"Soak 'em!" she calls out to the zombiefighters, opening the nozzle on the giant, truck-mounted chiller cannon.

The zombies *crash* into the unified streams of water coming from five equally powerful chiller cannons.

And then the mist erupts forth in such vast billowing clouds that whatever's happening in the struggle below is impossible to see. Even thermal goggles are useless—the steam is hot, and it's everywhere.

Chief Wachs settles her face mask into place and raises the collar on her zombieproof coat, as superheated blood and superchilled water collide.

24

NO WAY OUT

Regina finds Joule and Mrs. Artis together on the balcony that looked over the valley behind the house.

"This place is like if Frank Lloyd Wright designed zombieproof homes," Mrs. Artis remarks to Regina. "The only problem is that all the things that keep them out also keep you trapped inside. We need to be evacuating right now . . ."

"Mom—" Joule starts. But Mrs. Artis waves her off.

"I know you wish your father were here. I do, too. But I'm afraid you're stuck with me."

"Mom, *stop*," Joule cries.

Mrs. Artis closes her eyes, takes a deep breath, then exhales. "No one should have to live like this."

"Mrs. Artis?" Regina says. "My mom will be here soon. She promised she'd explain. She said not to go anywhere."

"But the evacuation—"

"She said to stay."

"I'm sorry, girls. I just don't know how this happened. How any of this happens. But I'm going to go inside and try to make some calls. Maybe someone else will have some answers."

With that, she goes inside. Regina doesn't think there's much chance of Mrs. Artis reaching someone who has the answers, but maybe that was just an excuse for wanting a little privacy.

Regina sees Joule's eyes tracing the path of the zombieproof wall and the rapidly flowing brook. An eyewateringly elegant and extraordinarily expensive zombie defense.

"Joule?" says Regina, sitting down with her friend.

Joule doesn't answer and just keeps staring out over the valley. The morning has brought a peculiar fog that blankets much of the city in the valley below. Making it look like they're sitting above the clouds. Only the giant coastal sequoias stick up above it all, like a fantasy world. It's surreal, especially where it collides with the orange Dusk—alien and harsh.

As they sit, the morning sun starts to work its way through patches of fog, revealing ruined rooftops. Chaotic, empty streets. And zombies.

So many zombies.

"We're evacuating, huh?" Joule says quietly.

"I guess so," Regina answers, even though she's still not sure what her mother has planned.

"That's all for Nelson Artis. I get it."

Regina hurts just watching what Joule's going through. But she embraces the ookyness. "I'm so sorry, Joule. I can't imagine . . . your dad is so awesome."

"You don't even know him."

"I do, and he's the best. He's stubborn, sure. But kind and caring. Selfless. And, like, weirdly funny. Everywhere he goes, everyone with eyes can see how great he is."

"How could you possibly have met my dad?"

"'Cause I met *you*, Joule," says Regina. "Nelson Artis is part of who you are, which makes him part of everything you do. I've known him since the moment you saved me from—from—"

"From a fate worse than death?" Joule suggests.

Regina smirks. "Now it's coming from your mouth, Joule! Oh my gosh. Seriously, clean yourself up, you're embarrassing yourself. So gross. Oh no, ew, it's coming out of your *eeeeeyes, Joule, nooo.*"

———

Joule is laughing, but what's going on inside her is more important.

She feels something crack open in her chest. Something that's been locked up has broken free. Something she's tried to protect, by hiding it from the world—

She's overwhelmed. All that joy that he's kindled inside her, by being her dad. Teaching her what it means, being alive. Having hope in the darkness.

Regina is right: It's all there.

———

They sit there together for what seems like a long time.

It's almost peaceful . . . until the security alarm goes off.

Regina and Joule rush to the security screens. A heavy-duty truck emblazoned with the HumaniTeam corporate logo is zooming up to the house, toward the zombies laying siege to the house. Regina and Joule watch as the truck stops just short of the running water in front of the closed drawbridge. Regina tenses as her mother steps out of the driver's seat, calmly opens the car door behind her, and takes out a chiller tank, aiming the nozzle and soaking the zombies to clear a path for the truck.

The frustrated, furious moans outside are so loud that Mrs. Artis comes running back into the room, asking what's going on.

Regina watches as her own mother, satisfied with the zombie stoppage, dumps the C-pack and gets back into the driver's seat. The bridge obediently lowers for her. Once it's retracting, she hits the garage door opener and drives in.

"Mom's home," Regina says.

25

UNTHINKABLE

When the horde and the brigade collide, boiling-hot steam fills the air.

It's only the brigadiers' protective clothing and enclosed helmets that save their lives. Instantly, they cover their faces with huge masks like those used in space suits, with oxygen tanks that keep the steam out of their mouths and lungs.

Thousands of zombies, strengthened by a night's fueling, pour into the city. The freeze trucks are rocked, and one of them is rolled onto its side, out of the fight.

Brigadiers scream and squirm free of the huge vehicle as its hose of supercooled water sprays out of control, hitting the freeze truck directly next to it.

Instantly, that second freeze truck is covered in a thick layer of ice, trapping the team of zombiefighters inside it.

The brigadiers work overtime to keep the purifying trucks feeding water to the remaining freeze trucks, while in the mobile command post, Chief Wachs has only two choices: Watch it happen, or abandon their positions and watch the city be torn apart.

Nix urges the others forward, confident that this city is already theirs. The chiller tanks have managed to hold back the horde's first crush, but they lost two of their trucks doing it.

If there's one thing that Nix has grown to appreciate in the past few hours, it's how incredibly strong the others have grown—after the long process of tunneling from the mine in the mountains, every part of their bodies is reinforced with minerals they dug through. The hunger that drives them on and on is magnified now by hands that cut like diamonds and bones that are unbreakable. Who knew that zombies could evolve like that?

These zombiefighters didn't. That's for certain.

As the zombie horde presses forward, another of the huge freeze trucks is defeated. It groans and tumbles into the river, its crew scurrying for safety wherever they can find it. Nix doesn't concentrate on that little detail. The horde has taken the bridge and now all that's left is to sweep the living aside.

In moments like this, they are all unified, working toward a goal that's larger than each individual's bottomless need.

And yet within Nix, somewhere, his own needs are languishing. Even as the living pour down a huge amount of cold water on the horde. Even as rank upon rank of zombies are sapped of strength, left unable to move, dissipated into nothingness, it is a different need that animates the zombie commander.

The need to not be alone. To find others like him. Caught in the gray space between monster and human.

She'll see that she belongs with him. Two outsiders, between living and undead.

Nix smiles and recklessly urges his forces forward.

When the city belongs to the horde, she'll have nowhere to run.

"We can't hold them with two freeze trucks, Chief."

"Yeah. Start pulling the support trucks out now. Keep the freeze trucks there until—"

A horrible sound interrupts Chief Wachs. A scream of agony that seems to come from everywhere at once.

In the command post, and among the trucks arrayed at the river's edge, everyone stops and turns toward it. Ears ringing—

With a terrible *crack*, one of the pillars of the steel bridge disintegrates as the whole structure on top of it tilts crazily, coming free of its supports. In the middle of the bridge, the decking breaks, sending zombies careening everywhere—backward onto the far bank, forward right up on top of the brigadiers, and also straight down into the river.

The brigadiers are stunned. Many of them start to cheer.

But Chief Wachs isn't among those who are cheering.

"Pack it up, folks! Quick, quick!"

The bridge itself begins to slide into the river, its metal bending and cracking. All the extreme heat of the zombies, all the extreme cold of the chillers—it has made the metal brittle. What would have taken decades or more to fail has happened over the course of fifteen minutes. It's astonishing, how much energy has been unleashed.

But there's no time to marvel.

"Let's get moving, folks!" says Chief Wachs. "Case you haven't noticed: We're on the wrong side of the river right now. Everybody over there with the zombies is totally on their own with a wave about to rebound on them."

26

FREE-FOR-ALL

Oliver feels stuck in the car, going slower than if they were walking. There's a ton of honking and shouting going on ahead of them. And though one or two jerks might get a car length ahead this way, in the end, it's only making everything go slower for everyone.

Oliver cranes his neck to try and see what's going on at the bridge, and Kirby watches him watching the battle.

And when Kirby sees him seeing her, her eyes go to the ground. There, on the carpet, is his notebook, which fell out of his back pocket. *Again.*

So he pins it against the seat with the heel of his shoe, scraping it up toward his hand. His sister looks confused, seeing the clear disrespectful treatment of the precious item.

A strange, enormous scream of metal comes from outside the car and Oliver drops the book right back on the floor. Del, who hasn't let go of his phone since his parents' call, grips it tighter.

Oliver rolls down his window to try and make out what's happening— superheated air comes in.

"Oliver, don't do that," his mother says as the air blast hits them. Hot beyond the thermometer's capacity to measure.

"Shh—I'm listening, Mom," Oliver says.

His heart leaps.

"They're cheering!" says Oliver. "The brigadiers! They're *winning*! Dad, you gotta stop. Turn around."

Oliver's dad looks in his rearview mirror, and rolls down his window, too, for a second before rolling it back up. Oliver looks to his mom and can see the tension in her face, and he can see the small relief she allows herself at this good news.

"Well, that's not nothing," she says. And that's it.

"That's all?" Oliver says.

"You gotta focus on the problem in front of you, Ollie. Give it all you got."

Oliver slams the back of his head into the seat again and again. He rolls up his window to block the stifling heat. The car continues to creep forward, inch by inch.

Doesn't matter, he decides. It'd be pretty much impossible for the Wachses' van to turn around on this road anyway, even if Oliver could make his parents listen to him.

As they keep rolling slowly forward, Oliver can feel the energy leaching out of him. The momentary thrill passes and leaves him even more hopeless. He's already lost everything, he remembers.

Except his family. He looks at Del and feels guilty, knowing his friend might be losing even more.

Ahead of them, the honking and screaming gets louder suddenly.

Oliver rolls his window down again.

"Oliver!" both his parents call back to him.

But all his attention is fixed on something outside.

"Uh, guys," he says, without fear, without shock.

Oliver's dad looks in the rearview mirror, and then opens his window to turn and stare.

The undead pour out of the shadows, falling from tree limbs like beetles landing on their backs and scurrying on without a second's hesitation. And the teamwork that he saw before? It's all gone now. These zombies are as eager to devour one another as they are to devour house after house, tree after tree. It's the terrible, unquenchable need that he's seen every zombie season since he can remember. Tearing through house after house—hungrier now than before. Hungrier now than *ever*.

"I don't—where did they all come from?" Oliver's mom wonders.

Amidst the leafy north side of the valley are orchards and pastures, all crawling with zombies. A herd of grazing sheep is more concerned with a coyote racing toward them. But their fear turns to confusion: The coyote flies past the herd and keeps going, jumping over the fence that marks the end of the pasture.

Slowly, the herd's relief fades as the sound of moaning from the trees grows louder. A patch of shadow seems to move slowly across the pasture. The sheep race off in the same direction as the coyote, but the fence is built to keep these sheep in, and it does its job well.

Orange eyes are the final thing they see—

These predators move up the hill, toward a line of cars that's hardly going anywhere at all.

At this point, no one is following the rules of the road. People are trying to drive on every patch of asphalt and flat grass available, but it's only making the logjam of cars harder and harder to move through.

"They're coming up the ridge!" Oliver says, even though everyone in the car can see it plain as day.

The traffic jam is an extremely effective barricade—only this barricade isn't keeping the zombies out. It's keeping the living in.

All around the Wachses' minivan, some people are getting out of their cars and running. Abandoning their cars wherever they are.

It's suddenly clear: It's everyone for themselves. A free-for-all.

"What do we do?" Oliver asks.

Nobody answers.

Farther up the line of cars, there are screeches of metal. People are actually driving into the cars around them! Meanwhile, Oliver's dad puts the car in park and thinks.

"What are you doing?!" Oliver demands. "We need to run. What are you *doing*?"

"Hold on, please!" his dad says.

162

Both his parents look around. On one side of the car is a steep sheet of rock. On the other side is a sharp slope downward. Pastures and orchards and creeks and parks—with who knows how many zombies.

"Oliver! I need you to help me," Dad says. He revs the engine and muscles the car through a gap between other cars, away from the rock. He drives it up over a curb, and the tires tear up the grass as the back wheels mount the sidewalk too.

"What???" he asks.

"Your maps, Ollie. Find me a path. The roads are closed, but your trails aren't. Get your notebooks and find me a way through."

"My maps? They're gone."

"What?" his mom says. "Of course they're not. They're in the back with your go bag. Some things are still important even when the situation is life and death."

Oliver looks at his mother like he's never seen her before.

"Remember when you asked me twelve hours ago, 'What are *you* doing?' Oliver? Right now we need you to find us a way clear of all this."

He starts to smile as he thinks about what they're about to attempt.

Then his smile fades.

All around them there are zombies. Screams come from farther ahead in the blocked chain of cars. This is not what he thought it would be. This is not a time when action is heroic. He remembers something else his father said, too, as it becomes clear that he was right: We are living with consequences, and there's very little we can do except deal with them, one at a time.

He finds his notebooks. They feel like an extension of himself. Something he had a nightmare of losing—but now he's awake and the relief is so real, it's mind-blowing.

He looks at Kirby, who silently locks eyes with him.

Focus on what you're doing right now, Oliver, he tells himself.

27

UNQUENCHABLE

Weakened and infuriated, the horde breaks apart.

Nix has lost control of them.

It's every zombie for themselves.

How did it happen?

Somehow, Nix has committed an unthinkable mistake. A mistake only a human would commit:

He underestimated his enemy . . .

Nix turns back to look up the hill, toward the house on the ridge.

And just as the others have broken apart, seeking fuel for themselves, Nix leaves the others behind.

She was so close to joining him, before.

This time he won't be caught off guard.

He races up the hill, marshaling a small cohort as he goes. Not a horde, but a horde isn't what he needs for this. He needs an elite team.

DUSK ALERT: SHELTER IN PLACE IMMEDIATELY. Due to a widespread emergency, all evacuation orders are CANCELED. Rogue Wave moving with unusual speed through a number of communities in California. Beware of treacherous conditions and sudden increases in zombie intensity! Get inside, and stay inside. The safest place is usually the lowest level, away from windows and doors.

Joule is shocked. This isn't the way things work. Once an evacuation is called, it never gets canceled—ever.

"Finally!" Dr. Herrera says under her breath as she reads the emergency alert on her phone. She looks up at the sky. Searching for something.

Joule shivers. She trusts Regina . . . but not her mother. Not one bit.

"What is it?" Regina says, and Joule hands her phone over, since Regina's is gone. After Regina reads the alert, she locks eyes with her mother.

"Is *this* part of your plan?" Regina asks her.

"Is what part of my plan?"

"This alert. You knew the evacuation was going to be canceled over an hour ago. What are you working on, Mom? Is this Coloma all over again?"

Coloma. Joule notices that Regina's voice shakes when she says it.

Dr. Herrera seems a little taken aback by Regina's intensity, her judgment. But she doesn't seem mad. She seems . . . ashamed. "We have a lot to talk about, Gina. But we need to get inside. Right now."

In the distance, a strange rumbling reaches their ears.

"Is that—?"

"Inside, please!" says Dr. Herrera sharply, her eyes on the dusk-red sky.

As Dr. Herrera leads them into the house, she continues looking up into nothingness.

Regina puts her hand on her mother's shoulder. "Are you okay?"

In reply she says "Help me with this?" as she begins covering the glass door with a curtain and pushing kitchen stools and other furniture against it.

"Why was the evacuation canceled?" Joule's mom asks. "Why did you tell us not to leave?" Outside, something hits the roof. "Was that a rock?"

"It's complicated," Dr. Herrera says. "They're canceling the evacuation because there's nowhere to go that's safer than here."

"Nowhere that's safer than the center of an uncontained zombie wave?"

Dr. Herrera nods gravely. "There are waves like this all over Northern California."

"How could they show up in all those places at once?" Joule's mom asks, barely holding herself together.

"It's a long story," says Dr. Herrera. "It involves an abandoned mine and a misguided attempt to make zombies useful by using them to power a generator."

"So the rumors are *true*?" says Joule, looking from Dr. Herrera to Regina and back again.

"There's a kernel of truth to them, yeah," says Dr. Herrera. "But the full story is a lot more complicated, and I've been trying to get a handle on it for months. I—"

Regina glares at her mother. She heads out to barricade the other windows as Dr. Herrera continues.

"It's even worse, other places," Dr. Herrera explains. "Sacramento, Lake Tahoe, everything up there—they got hit even faster, harder. Didn't even get the warning, before . . . the wave started building underground, so there wasn't any warning. No good options."

They continue to barricade the windows of the house until it feels like a dark cavern. Joule can't help but wonder what will happen if the electricity goes out.

"Everyone just meet back in the kitchen!" Dr. Herrera calls. "I'll tell you whatever I can."

But when Joule and her mother meet back as Dr. Herrera told them to, Regina has gone missing.

"Where'd she go?" Dr. Herrera asks.

Joule checks their room.

Not there.

When she returns to the kitchen to tell Dr. Herrera this, she tries to cover any alarm. Regina wouldn't slip away now, not when Dr. Herrera was about to answer all her questions.

"The house isn't that big," Dr. Herrera says. "Let's split up and look for her."

Joule and her mother glance around and they go to look—

"Regina?!"

They can't find her on the main floor of the house.

They all spread out.

On a hunch, Joule goes back to Regina's room . . . and stops short. This time the window is fully open. A hot wind is gusting in through it. And a memory floods her mind, unbidden. A zombie in the distance, crooking a finger toward Regina.

"In here!" she calls, a terrible feeling in her stomach.

Joule's mom arrives first and instantly goes to stand with her daughter, not allowing her anywhere near the open window. When Dr. Herrera enters, she's wearing the C-pack from the truck in the garage. She looks ready for anything.

"What's going on, Joule?" she asks.

As Joule looks from the open window to Dr. Herrera and back again, Dr. Herrera's expression shifts uncertainly.

"I don't know," Joule says. "There was a—I don't know how to—" Joule just stares at Regina's mother with a panicked astonishment.

Dr. Herrera braces herself for anything and steps through the window onto the precarious slope of the roof underneath its lip. "Regina?!"

Joule tries to follow, and her mother blocks her.

Dr. Herrera locks eyes with Mrs. Artis.

Mrs. Artis wraps an arm around Joule.

"Barricade this window when I'm out," Dr. Herrera commands as she heads out to look for her daughter.

28

AN ATLAS AT LAST

"Left! No— I meant next left—*hold on*." Oliver flips a few pages in his notebook as the Wachses' car crashes through a woodland trail into a sheep pasture. "Yeah, okay, good! We're okay, keep going this way."

Oliver Wachs has officially become a human GPS navigation system.

It hasn't been smooth, but the zombies have all been too surprised to see them crash through the brush to do much more than swivel their heads to watch.

"I'm not sure how much trail we've got left ahead of us."

"Give me what you can, Ollie," his father says.

Ollie grins through the fear and exhaustion.

"Wait! There's the community pool up here if you go left left left! No, Dad, LEFT!"

"You refused to go the beach, but now you wanna go lie around at the pool?"

"I want to jump in there where the zombies can't go."

"Oh. Yeah, that's—hold on!"

Six zombies stumble right into the car's path and Oliver's dad has to veer crazily around them, sending the car skidding in a cloud of dust—

He turns the wheel into the skid, and the car straightens, though the dust is still everywhere— "You see what I just did there, Oliver? You remember that when you're learning to drive! Which way to the pool?"

"Uhhh, straight!"

"Straight?"

"Straight!"

"Can't go straight," his mom calls out. Oliver looks up from the map and sees why. The woods ahead are crawling with zombies.

One of them rips open the hood of the car and reaches for the engine parts inside. Oliver's dad presses the gas pedal hard, and then jams on the brake, sending the zombie backward onto the ground.

"Kids, you get out and run for the pool, and you *jump in* and stay there. Okay?"

"Mom!"

"Do it, Oliver! This is not the time to argue!!" His mother turns around to look at them, and seeing her face, Oliver's eyes fill with hot tears.

Then the front windshield spiderwebs with the impact of a fist, once, twice—

"Go, kids!"

Oliver looks at his sister. Kirby is staring at him. Del is curled in a ball.

A dozen more fists hit the car. Then even more than that. It's impossible to count. It's too late to run. *This is it*, he realizes. The zombies are going to peel apart the car and devour every piece of it, and the people inside.

And as he lets it sink into him that this is the end, Oliver feels . . . silly. Small. Sad.

Kirby reaches over and takes his hand.

Like a rope around his waist as he's falling off a cliff, her hand holds him fast, and keeps him from falling.

In mid-tumble, between light and dark—furious over losing "everything" while completely blind to the intact family and friends who surround him even now. Even in this car, as the end nears.

"Thanks, Kirby," Oliver says, grateful beyond words to have a sister with a heart like hers. *Some things are still important even when it's life and death,* he thinks.

He's sure that she can't hear his words, over the percussive calamity. But she can read his thoughts clear as day. For Oliver, this revelation comes without a moment to spare: The blows that fall on the car have begun to pierce the metal, coming in on all sides . . .

29

NELSON ARTIS WAS HERE

Joule and her mother are alone in a palace, with the windows barricaded up except for the skylights that they could not reach, as the fog has given way to an unsettling darkness in the sky above.

Joule watches the security camera monitors, seeking any clues about what has happened to Regina. She remembers the look the zombie gave her friend—a combination of hunger and fascination—and wonders whether that should be a comfort or a reason to be even more terrified.

At the kitchen table, Mrs. Artis sits, staring at her phone. Scrolling. Its glowing screen casts her features in an eerie light.

Joule peers closer to get a look at what's on the screen. Family pictures, she sees.

"Mom?" says Joule.

Joule's mom puts down the phone and meets Joule's eye. For a long moment, neither of them speaks. Then Joule breaks the silence, stumbling through an apology for running away. "I'm sorry. I didn't do it to hurt you."

"I know, Jouley-bean," her mother says. "But it's just you and me now. We have to have each other's backs."

Joule realizes she and her mother have both spent their anger already, and now the dust is settling. The air is clearer.

"Also," her mom continues, "I didn't do a great job planning our move to New York, I guess. I didn't mean to make it so scary."

"*Moving* isn't scary," Joule says. "It's . . . What if he's out there, part of that wave—right now? Trapped away in some corner of himself, screaming to be set free? *That's* what scares me."

Joule's mother takes this in, silently.

"Don't you ever think about what it's like for them all, Mom? Losing who you are?"

"Is that what you believe?"

Joule gives the most honest answer she has. "I don't know what to believe." A lot has happened in the last few hours. And though it's unsettling, and intolerable, sitting in the safety of this fortresslike home while there's horror and pain everywhere, her mind is quieter now. She thinks about her father as part of the horde of destructive zombies, screaming to be free. She closes her eyes and listens. Not wanting to hear him, but actually listening. And in a corner of her own mind, there's a little voice that's been screaming for her attention, and finally ensnares her.

Hello?

It's the voice of her dad.

We traced the call, Miss Artis. It's coming from inside the house!

What a dumb joke, she tells herself.

But it makes her smile, despite everything. *Because* of everything.

He's been trying to get her attention for a very long time, trapped not in the corner of a zombie's useless brain but in a corner of *her* mind, waiting to be freed. For two hundred sleeps. An entire autumn, winter, and spring.

I'm right here, Joule. The words well up inside her. *Anytime you don't know what to believe in. I'm always right here, to tell you what I believe in is you.*

Joule feels herself missing him even more than ever, as his words reverberate like a song. It's a breaking point, and a new beginning, and she holds on to the feeling as long as she can.

Eventually, Joule remembers the presence of her mother by her side. Continuing to wait. Patient. Well, mostly patient.

And suddenly a new surge of emotions swells inside her. Something urgent. And impossible to satisfy.

Joule throws her arms around her mother. Squeezing. Hard.

"I'm ready when you are, Mom," says Joule.

Joule's mother just squeezes her back, and doesn't say anything right away.

30

UNSPEAKABLE

It was inevitable.

Nix had already found Regina once tonight. Some part of her had always known that he'd come back for her again.

And that the next time, he wouldn't leave empty-handed.

She was prepared for it, but it was still a shock to see a looming figure standing in the shadowy corner of her bedroom—in the Project Coloma jacket, with the unreadable, orange, empty eyes. She was going to break him into a thousand pieces and scatter them from a plane.

She eyed the superchiller Joule had left by the bed and inched toward it.

It made her shiver when he said, "It's time for you to come where you belong."

"Looks to me like you're not going to give me any choice," Regina said, her anger coming fast and hot.

"You're not like the others . . . I see it. So do you."

It was still unbelievable to her, to hear words come out of his mouth. It went against everything she'd ever learned about zombies.

And if that one thing was wrong . . . what else didn't she know?

"You're like me," said Nix. "You understand."

She tried not to show her uncertainty to Nix. She was still pretty sure he was a foe, even if he was talking like a friend.

"See for yourself," the zombie said, half commanding and half pleading.

The words made Regina's temper flare.

No, Regina thought. *I'm not like you.*

But as she took another step toward the chiller, Nix crossed the room suddenly and grabbed the weapon, holding it up with disdain, a sound of fury coming from his throat as he hurled it across the room and wrapped his arms around her waist, heaving her over his shoulder as he rushed out the window and jumped down to the ground below. His grasp was strong; her ribs felt like they were bending and all the air was pushed from her lungs.

She tried shouting for help. Her mother would make it outside in five seconds flat. But Nix held her so tight that she couldn't breathe. In her dwindling vision, she saw the other figures lurking in the darkness, half-concealed in the hedges lining the yard. *How?*

A number of trees had been torn down and carried to form a bridge over the running water and up to the top of the protective wall.

Regina marveled as another tree was carried over the bridge, and dropped to the ground inside the wall, for Nix to use to carry Regina back out again.

Plan.

Regina made a quick calculation:

Her mom, Joule, and Joule's mom would be outnumbered.

By about twenty to one.

That's when she knew: Even if she could shout for her mom, she couldn't summon her into this trap.

If there was a way out, Regina would have to find it on her own.

———————

Nix remains silent as he leads her across the tree-bridge. His hand will not leave her arm. His skin is so hot it leaves a burn, but that doesn't concern Regina—it comforts her. *See? I'm not like you, Nix*, she thinks.

She studies the way the other zombies are looking to him to take the lead. Like they're an army and he's the general.

Interesting.

"What now, Nix?" she asks. "I'm here. What do you expect to happen now?"

For some reason, she's not afraid anymore. Maybe because she already knows the answer: Just as the other zombies have their needs driving them—their hollowness—Nix has a hollowness of a different kind. The hollowness of being truly alone in the world. He needs a partner. A friend.

"You gotta say it, Nix."

She sees he's unwilling. She's asking him for something that makes him feel weak. Vulnerable. And she *is* asking him for that.

He's not entirely wrong about her—she's brave enough to confess that to herself. It's upsetting for Regina to make herself remember what happened in the woods, before Joule saved her life. How she *was* one of them.

Nix is still trapped in that same kind of twilight, she can see now. For him the difference between being alive and being undead isn't like a light switch that turns on or off. It's more like a slow fading from brightness to darkness.

Curious, she keeps focused on Nix, putting pieces of a jigsaw puzzle together in her mind: *How does he know how to talk?*

The part of her that delights in solving puzzles, that muscle that works with such quiet focus that sometimes it's impossible to notice, pushes something up from inside her.

"Project Coloma isn't the only way HumaniTeam is experimenting with zombies, is it?" Her eyes move to the patch on his jacket and she slowly regains her breath. "They tried to experiment on you, didn't they? Project Nix? Project *Phoenix*, maybe?"

He doesn't respond, but she persists.

"What was it supposed to do? Turn you into a productive member of society or something? And then, when it didn't 'work'—they dropped you back into a dark place where they were sure you'd be destroyed. But you weren't."

The zombie looks back at her, his hands clamped into fists.

Shaking.

Then—

He raises the fist, and it bobs forward. Like a head nodding.

Yes.

Regina smiles. Without joy; more like sadness. But in that uncomfortable feeling there is . . . . understanding. Connection. Empathy. "We *could* all use more friends," Regina says carefully. "But you can't take friendship from someone by force, Nix."

Without a move, without a look, the zombies that surround Nix all turn their backs and drift away, leaving them alone together.

"Then . . . how?" he asks.

She doesn't know the answer, she discovers.

She can see the not-quite-zombie sink into himself.

Then there's a sound from the sky, and Nix's eyes go straight up.

Regina follows his gaze and sees—

From the sky comes a sound and a sight far more unexpected in California than zombies are. A dark, green-gray thunderstorm is pushing through the red dusk sky. A bone-shaking thunderclap vibrates through Regina's chest, and the entire valley where the city rests.

Nix looks at her as a raindrop hits him and hisses to steam. No: not a raindrop.

Ice. The ground at her feet is pocked with quarter-sized chunks of ice.

Up and down the landscape, ice is falling from the sky. Striking the earth with loud bangs. Bouncing back five feet into the air. It's a hailstorm.

"Regina?!"

It's a familiar voice. Regina's mother's voice.

"Run," Regina tells Nix.

"Regina, get down!" Her mother comes over the tree-bridge, a C-pack on her back, its nozzle aimed at Nix.

Regina spins back around, but Nix hasn't moved at all.

"Run, Nix!" she says, putting herself in front of the zombie. "Hold on, Mom!" Regina's eyes meet her mother's. Regina can see her confusion and intense fear.

Then, as her mother's eyes shift to look behind Regina, Regina turns around. Nix is fleeing, ducking under cover both from Dr. Herrera's superchiller and the ice that's begun to pound down around them, all across the city.

"Under the bridge!" Dr. Herrera says to Regina, pointing to the tree-bridge she just crossed over.

Regina nearly gets hit in the head by a fist-sized chunk of ice, and in a dazed state makes it under cover, even as the hailstorm grows ferociously . . .

31

LOST AND FOUND

Nix darts through the hailstones, using his rugged jacket with its Project Coloma patch to shield him from the storm.

As the zombie general flees, all around him zombies are being extinguished—struck by ice chunks, swept up in the new rivers forming everywhere.

For Nix, the unstoppable power of water is hypnotizing.

The chill of it steals into him even without touching his skin. It takes all his strength and cleverness to stay safe.

And because he's focusing on this effort, he doesn't notice the rapidly growing flood of icy water on the ground. Not until it pours into his boots and each foot goes cold and useless. There's no fighting this, no retreat from it.

Panicking, he stops in place.

Almost instantly, the superheated blood flowing in his veins makes the water flash to steam and rise up around his ankles. It leaves Nix shaken. He is extremely eager to get out of this awful place.

Empty inside, all he has the energy to do is to limp into the wilderness and delve down into a barrow, where he will lie silent for the next thousand years. Until all of what's happened here in Redwood is ancient history. Until . . . until . . .

As the ice storm keeps coming, Nix realizes that what happens next is out of his control.

All he wanted was to find a friend.

You can't take friendship from someone by force, Nix.

Regina's words live on in his head, the only voice within the emptiness.

He feels it eating him up from the inside, its teeth sharp and long.

Why do I feel like this?

So much easier to not have any words to explain his feelings.

Much easier to be one of the horde, even if right now that leads to destruction.

Suddenly, Nix can feel a presence in the water, moving toward him. Something hungry. Something that moves with purpose, with black-hole hunger.

It shouldn't be possible. But it's there.

In the water, plunging through it—everywhere and nowhere—is a zombie horde unlike any other he has ever known.

32

THE UNNATURAL DISASTER AREA

The Wachses' minivan creaks and groans as it rocks from side to side. Inside the car, the windows are spiderwebbed with so many cracks that they've turned almost opaque.

Oliver can hear his mother screaming his name, but it sounds faint and distant. Like she's calling to him from very far away instead of the front seat. But all Oliver can focus on are his sister and Del. Thinking about all those evenings "playing" Manhunt. Wishing he'd caught more grasshoppers with Kirby instead. While the game might have been teaching him how to not die in a world where zombies are everywhere, it made him forget that there's a huge difference between *how to not die* and *how to live*.

"Kirby?" The van is coming apart, but the intense fury of the horde hasn't consumed them yet. In fact, for reasons that are unclear, the air has gone a little cold.

She wraps him in a hug, and he squeezes her back.

There's a cataclysmic *boom* outside the van.

A bone-shaking thunderclap vibrates through the car, and Oliver's chest, and the entire valley where the city rests. Suddenly, Oliver realizes why it's cold: The blows hitting the car aren't zombie punches.

It's ice. From the sky. Big chunks of ice—

"Kirby!" says Oliver. "It's a thunderstorm." He releases his sister, and jogs his mother's shoulder, as she strains to see through the cracked windshield. Del seems to retreat further into himself. Oliver's dad grips the wheel hard.

As the storm grows and grows, Oliver tries to press his eye up to the spider-webbed window. His mother pulls him back. "Careful, honey," she says.

Oliver's grin is huge. "You gotta see this."

He pulls on the door of the minivan, to reveal what's outside. The little motor inside gallantly insists on opening it for him—and since the track's gotten banged up, it jams halfway—but the view is clear. Outside the van, the swarm is broken. The zombies have been stopped in their tracks.

"How?" says Oliver's mother.

Oliver gently pushes against the window, and the whole panel falls to the ground, along with a thick coating of ice—

Kssssh!

Cool, wet air hits his nose, face, and tongue. Wordlessly, Kirby joins him.

"Come on," Oliver tells Del. "It's okay."

But Del shakes his head. Checks his phone again. Refuses to leave the van.

Oliver and Kirby watch the hushed landscape. Momentarily, it has become winter. Completely calm, like just after a blizzard. There are inches of ice on the ground. Big chunks of hail, all fused together into a frozen bumpy crust. But even now the ice is melting as all the heat makes a foggy, soupy mess.

Kirby grabs her brother's arm and points with the other toward something in the distance.

From the fog, two figures emerge.

"There's someone out there," says Oliver to their parents. "Hey, Mom, Dad—look."

"I see 'em," says Oliver's mother. "Looks like they need help."

They stumble closer. Clearly a couple.

"Mom? Dad?" Del says, dropping his phone. Before Oliver can stop him, he's out the door.

"Get back in here!" Oliver's dad calls out.

But Del's not listening.

He doesn't know how they found him, but they have. Tears blur his eyes as he runs to them as fast as he can.

Oliver runs after him, tries to slow him down.

Because as he gets closer, he realizes the adult figures aren't Del's parents. They're—

"Zombie. *Zombie!*" Oliver calls out.

Behind him, he hears the van roar to life. He turns and sees his dad gunning toward them, his mom and sister leaning out the open door.

"Jump!" his mom calls.

It's against everything his parents have ever taught him to jump into a moving vehicle, but that's what he does, Kirby yanking him in. He looks out and sees his mom reaching for Del, about to fall out of the van. Del looks paralyzed—he's realized what's right in front of him. Oliver's mom grabs at him and misses. The zombies reach and their fingers are inches away from having Del. With a scream of rage, Oliver's father yanks the steering wheel, and the front of the van goes crashing into the distracted zombies. Their bodies thud against the windshield in a burst of gore and heat.

The van then screeches to a halt. Del has fallen to the ground. "Stay here!" Oliver's mom orders, then runs out and carries Del back into the van. They try to shut the door, but it's stuck.

Then there's a groan. From under the van.

A zombie groan.

"Drive! Go go go!" Oliver cries.

33

JUST THE BEGINNING

Under the tree-bridge, Regina and her mother hold tight to each other as the hailstorm wraps trees in icicles and pulls their branches off every bit as well as zombies do. Knocking holes in windows, filling homes with six inches of ice within five minutes.

And then it stops.

The wave is spent, and so is the storm.

"Wow," says Regina as she stands and looks out into the world, all its furious zombie activity now stilled. All that remains of the wave is an army of frozen figures. Superheated blood sapped of all warmth.

"Well, that's that," says Dr. Herrera wearily.

Regina looks back at her. "Mom? What just happened?"

"This is Project Cloudbuster."

"This is what you've been working on, since . . ."

"Yeah." Dr. Herrera's silence stretches a long time, as she comes out to look at the world beside her daughter. Dr. Herrera seems a little numb, her eyes slightly red around the edges. "It's shocking how much energy there is in a little bit of water, isn't it?"

"Yeah." Regina doesn't know what else to say to this. For one thing, her mother looks defeated, not victorious. "What's wrong, Mom?"

Dr. Herrera eyes Regina from head to toe, her lips tightly pressed together. "What were you doing out here, Gina?" she asks wearily.

Regina looks at her mother, a giant lump in her throat. She doesn't know how to make the words come; it feels like trying to eat a rock.

"It's hard to explain, Mom."

"It's been a lot," Dr. Herrera says. "It's okay. *You're* okay."

Regina wants to tell her mother everything, but it's impossible to put her words in any kind of logical order. She remembers herself falling into that the twilight between human and zombie, like Nix. She imagines herself out there, like him. Chased, hunted. And amidst that doubt, Regina feels the dam inside her start to leak, and words start to come out.

"Mom, there's something . . . there's something weird going on at HumaniTeam. Something . . . that the company isn't being honest about."

Dr. Herrera raises her eyebrows in surprise. "I'm sorry?"

"I was . . . I've been trying to prove that the accident at the mine wasn't your fault. That your generator worked . . ."

"You did *what*?"

"Please don't get mad, I just—"

"How long have you been . . . looking into this matter, Regina?"

"Mom, please."

"Since the Event . . . ?"

Regina looks at the ground and nods.

Dr. Herrera sighs heavily. "Gina, I wish you'd talked to me."

"You would have stopped me."

"Well. Yeah. But I *might* have also told you that you're right."

Regina's eyes snap up again. "I was?"

Dr. Herrera hesitates, then closes her eyes and rubs her temples. "Well. I suppose it doesn't matter if I talk about it now. It's too late to do anything." Dr. Herrera takes the C-pack off her back and holds it in her hands. "I have *also* spent every day since the Event digging and digging to find out what's been secretly going on at HumaniTeam."

"You know about . . . the ways that HumaniTeam is experimenting on zombies?"

"I . . ." Dr. Herrera pauses, considering this. "What do you mean experimenting?"

"Project Phoenix?" says Regina.

"What is 'Project Phoenix'?" Dr. Herrera asks, her confusion genuine.

"It's HumaniTeam's project to try and make smart zombies," says Regina.

Dr. Herrera's eyes widen slightly. "Smart. Zombies."

"That's the reason they're acting weird out there in this wave, I think. That zombie you just saw me with? He's, like, like their commander or something."

"But you were trying to stop me from extinguishing him," Dr. Herrera says.

"He's . . . he's . . . not all bad, Mom. He's . . . trying." Regina hesitates. "Hold on. What exactly did you *think* I was talking about?"

"We're not done talking about this Project Phoenix. But right now, we do have a more immediate problem. We need to warn people about all the damage that Project Cloudbuster just did."

"Damage?" Regina asks. "Like the broken windows?"

Dr. Herrera lets out a bitter laugh. "No, not the windows."

"Mom, spill it."

"Regina, HumaniTeam has been hiding a big problem with the super-chillers they build." She brandishes the chiller tank in her hands. "Everybody on the planet sees them as a modern miracle. Guaranteed to stop a zombie in fifteen seconds. Drain all the heat from their blood. Fully extinguished. And Project Cloudbuster is based on the same concept, only a million times bigger. It takes an astonishing amount of energy to stop a zombie. Each one of these chillers in the world uses more energy than a gasoline engine running all day."

"But . . . it worked?" says Regina. "The zombies were—"

"That's only how it looks on the surface. HumaniTeam has gone to extraordinary lengths to hide the truth that superchillers are actually making the zombies *much* worse."

As soon as Dr. Herrera says this, it clicks. It fits with all the rest of what she learned these past few months about how they are dishonest about their failures, blinded by their big dreams.

Suddenly, Regina realizes that all around them, the ice is *really* melting. It's flowing into the rollicking creek that flows right next to them, turning it into a whitewater rapid.

"What just happened here, it's like a million superchillers' worth of damage that just got done in an instant, and it's also happening in a bunch of other places facing other tentacles of this Rogue Wave. There are going to be really big consequences, I'm afraid."

"Mom, I think we should get inside the house?"

Dr. Herrera keeps her eyes locked on Regina, even as Regina's attention darts around, alarmed at the power of the melting water all around. For a moment out of reality, the creek is overflowing its banks and gushing water pours out everywhere, eroding the soft ground next to the wall.

"In a minute, Regina. I'm standing right here and not moving an inch until I'm a hundred percent sure that you know, down to your bones, that you didn't cause *any* of what's happening out there right now. You did nothing but insist to *help*. To have a voice, in the decisions about the world you were born into. And I can hear that voice, loud and clear. *You* are all I care about."

"I get it, Mom, can we *go*?"

Dr. Herrera makes no move to go inside.

The water is furiously grasping, pulling, scraping . . . like it's got a mind of its own. And as Regina watches, mesmerized . . .

Something lifts itself up out of the water.

A zombie. An *extinguished*, waterlogged zombie. Its eyes no longer orange, but an unfathomable, watery dark. It fumbles, reaching awkwardly toward Regina's mother.

Regina picks up the superchiller that her mother dropped and aims the nozzle at the zombie.

"Regina, don't!" calls out Dr. Herrera.

The warning comes too late. Regina opens the hose and releases a powerful lance of superchilled water that hits the zombie in the chest.

But the water doesn't flash to steam when it hits the unnatural monstrosity.

The zombie simply absorbs the blast into itself. *Fueling* it. Making it stronger. *Larger*. Regina looks from the monster to her mother, blinking, trying to understand what she's just seen.

"Gina, this is what I've been trying to tell you. The superchillers don't always work the way we expect them to against the zombies. Not anymore."

Regina's mother grabs her arm and yanks her up onto the tree-bridge even as the wall groans and cracks under the weight, its foundations weakened by the water.

They're only just over the wall when it falls inward after them, the newborn monster surging forward as it finds its footing in the churning water, swelling still larger, raging as it devours everything that flows into this new lake it inhabits: mud and sticks and the bodies of the zombies whose superheated blood did not withstand the Cloudbuster's power.

Regina tears herself away long enough to glance at her mother.

There's a terrible pain in Dr. Herrera's eyes.

34

A GIANT PROBLEM

Inside the Herreras' zombieproof home, Joule and her mother listen to the silence in the wake of the hailstorm, still holding each other with a fierce intensity. High above, the skylight is broken, its glass scattered across the kitchen, but the air that flows in feels humid.

"It's over, Mom." Joule relaxes her grip on her mother and moves to the barricaded rear face of the house.

"Joule?" says her mother. "Keep away from that. It's not safe."

But Joule doesn't retreat. She pulls away pieces of the furniture blocking her from seeing what's happened. The expensive, zombieproof glass is still intact, and through it she can see into a bank of cotton-like cloud, swiftly drifting up from the ground and kiting across the valley sky. She wonders where Regina and her mother went—whether they found a place to shelter somewhere else in the house, or whether they fled, leaving Joule and her mother on their own. *No, Regina wouldn't have done that*, Joule thinks to herself. She's so honest, so passionate about what she believes. And she knows Regina wouldn't have abandoned her.

"Joule, please. Let's just wait for some kind of all clear."

"I want to see what's out there, Mom. I won't go anywhere."

Before Joule's mother can reply, there's an immense, rattling crash from the front of the house. The door stays locked and braced, even as moisture seeps in around every edge, pooling on the floor inside the door.

"On second thought," Joule's mother says. "Let me help you with that."

Quickly, they tear away the remains of the improvised barricade against the door that leads to the back porch.

Another blow against the front of the house leaves the entire front of the building leaking water across the floor. On the third crash, the front door finally comes free of its hinges and barrels down the hall, right at the Artises.

A wall of water follows it. But not just water. There is mud and there are sticks, even a broken tree that Joule recognizes as being very recently deeply rooted outside Regina's window.

Then there's something else.

A huge, bloated monstrosity.

A giant zombie. Twelve feet tall, and very nearly just as wide around.

Carried in by rush of the water.

"Get out, Joule!" her mom shrieks, throwing herself in front of her daughter.

Joule squeezes her eyes shut and for one brief, ridiculous moment, she feels like this is all a dream. That she's a little kid again and nothing can hurt her while her mom is there.

But then the cold water hits her ankles, jerking her back to reality.

"We're both getting out, Mom!" Joule calls, grabbing her mother's hand. They half run, half stagger down the hall and wrench open the partially unbarricaded back door that leads out onto the porch overlooking the sheer drop into the valley below.

The raging giant chases them, sweeping through the house. The enormous zombie's hunger only grows with each new item it consumes as it charges ahead.

It grasps the table, the refrigerator, the walls of the house itself—

It gets bigger and bigger.

More and more massive.

Its weight is unstoppable.

The giant monstrosity slams into the back door that Joule and her mother exited through, and that entire wall pulls free of the rest of the house. It's sliding toward the edge, toward the cliff.

All that weight and speed is working against it now, Joule realizes, with a sudden rush of hope.

"Get out of its path! It's going over the cliff!"

"What?" her mother asks, turning to face Joule.

As Joule and her mother are locked, eye to eye, the zombie reaches . . .

It grabs Joule's mother by the leg.

"MOM!" Joule screams. Joule reaches for her mother and grabs the edge of her shirt with all her strength.

The zombie keeps pulling her mother in the other direction, pulling her closer to the edge of the steep cliff. "NO!" Joule shouts. She digs her heels into the ground . . . leans all the way back, using her entire body weight to counteract the deadly force.

But it's not enough. Nothing Joule does is ever enough.

The zombie and her mother tumble off the edge of the bluff, into the fog.

A moment later, the ground shakes from an impact far below.

And Joule feels her heart shatter.

"Mom?" she whispers as tears begin to stream down her cheeks. "Mom, please . . . no . . ."

A cavity opens in her chest, darker and more gaping than any zombie barrow. Like the hollowness she felt after her dad's disappearance. It expands and expands. Filling her with emptiness.

"Mom!!" Joule calls out once more, leaning into the fog.

"I'm here!" Her mother's voice is so close it startles her.

"MOM?" Joule repeats, certain she imagined the voice, bracing for another walloping of pain.

"We're going to the airport *right* now, Joule," says Mrs. Artis, crawling into view, clinging to the limbs of a proud, tall coastal redwood fifteen feet below.

"Mom!" Joule shouts, and suddenly it's the most joyful word in the world. "Are you okay?"

"I'm fine," her mother says. "I just need to figure out a way off this thing."

"Just stay there, I'm coming for you," Joule says with a laugh that's also part sob.

"Joule? Mrs. Artis?" The voice of Regina Herrera precedes her as she climbs through the brand-new zombie-shaped hole in the side of her "totally zombieproof" house.

"Hi, Regina!" Mrs. Artis calls out brightly. "You have, like, a rope or something in there that I can borrow for a minute?"

"Uh, I think so?" Regina surveys the situation with concern. "Hold tight!"

Regina, Joule, and Dr. Herrera quickly come up with a plan, employing a ladder whose rungs form a perfect set of stairs from the house to the tree, and a thick climbing rope for safety.

When all four of them are together in the ruined kitchen, Mrs. Artis does the only sensible thing in this situation and portions out the cold coffee left in the bottom of the coffee machine.

"What now?" Joule asks.

"Now we save lives, if we can," says Dr. Herrera, holding her phone to her ear, frustrated. "People need to get to higher ground, right now."

"Who are you calling, Mom?" Regina asks.

Far down in the valley, Chief Wachs sees Dr. Herrera's number come up on her screen and ignores the call.

"All right, everyone! We got this, don't let up now!"

She returns to focusing on her two remaining freeze trucks, which are still pouring supercooled water on the extinguished zombies, shoving them all into the river that will sweep them out to the Pacific Ocean, where they'll be permanently trapped, cold and unable to harm anyone.

"Answer it, Chief," Dr. Herrera pleads, hitting redial.

It only rings and rings, as Chief Wachs ignores the call . . .

"We can't just let other people be surprised like we were," says Regina. "We need to tell people the truth."

"Yes," Dr. Herrera agrees. "But I've lost all my friends now, it appears."

She looks deeply shaken. Drawn and weary.

The phone continues to ring.

Regina looks at Joule, grateful for her friendship. For helping restore a part of her soul she didn't even know was withering away.

Regina thinks back to the night before, and it feels like a different lifetime: the terror of meeting Nix; Joule saving Regina's life at the last possible moment; turning back to face danger once again to help her friends Darlene and Chanda and the other boy. The clever one, who found her phone and outran the zombies.

I've lost all my friends now, it appears. Her mother's words echo as Chief Wachs ignores her call.

In the back of her mind, something dings. Chief *Wachs*. And the boy who was with Darlene and Chanda . . .

"Ollie," says Regina.

Regina stiffens, tilting her head. Looking at Joule.

"What?" says Joule.

"Ollie *Wachs*."

35

RAPIDS

Lurking in the rushing waters, Nix can feel three individual, powerful hungers. But they don't need a leader like him to help them feed. They're each as strong as a small horde, and they'd just as soon tear Nix apart and eat him if he got in their path.

He hears an unexpected, human voice. "Drive! Go go go!"

Nix lifts his head and sees a minivan, with the back door open. Two zombie bodies lie by the van. One isn't moving. The other is pushing itself up from the muck under the van, drowning as the waters flood in. As Nix turns, the human boy in the minivan sees his nightmare-like face. "Zombie. Zombie! Dad, drive!"

The wheels spin, but the van doesn't move. It is engulfed in water.

In the rapids, the cold hungers are grasping for the van, holding it back as it tries to surge forward.

Amidst this, Nix feels the watery, hungry creature's claws sink into his leg. Raking. An icy chill follows, running up the veins of his leg.

The Wachs family van struggles to get traction in the rushing water, and Oliver gets a wild idea.

"Dad!" he calls out. "Go with the flow!"

"What?" he says, in disbelief.

"First rule of zombie season. When in doubt, go with the flow!" Oliver grabs his box of notes and maps, and rifles through it, searching, searching. "Yes!" he cries, holding aloft a rolled-up sheet of paper near the bottom. "Remember last year when we got that big rainstorm?"

"Not even a little bit," says Oliver's mom.

"Neither did I—that's why I wrote it down."

"Skip to the point, kiddo," says Oliver's mom. "Kirby, what are you doing?" she adds, seeing Kirby move closer to the open door of the minivan.

Oliver doesn't watch what his sister is doing, he just calls out to his mom: "If you want to get out of this alive, you need to put the van in reverse right now! We need to go *with* the current—let the water take us, get up some speed, and gun the engine to get out of it."

"Yeah, Oliver, *okay* . . ." his dad says.

"I'm serious! You have a better plan?"

Oliver's dad's expression goes from dismissal to disbelief to determination. He locks eyes for a moment with Oliver's mom, then says, "Yeah, okay—okay, yeah." He reverses the van, and hits the gas. Del, already curled up in shell shock, curls up further.

Meanwhile, Kirby looks out the open door of the minivan at the zombie boy whose feet are touching the rushing floodwater, hissing with steam. Quietly, she says, "Wait."

No one notices her.

"Wait!" Kirby croaks, louder.

Surprised to hear Kirby's voice raised, her father looks back and lets his foot off the gas, just for a moment . . .

Kirby has reached her arm out of the car, her palm open, grasping for the zombie's arm. As her fingers close, she winces and makes a sound of pain.

"Kirby?!" Oliver cries, grabbing his sister with both arms, as the zombie grasps her arm right back.

"Dad, we need to go!" Oliver shouts, even though the wheels are already spinning as fast as they can, spitting mud everywhere as Oliver's parents both spit curses even faster. As the van zooms forward, Kirby is pulled, but Oliver grabs her and holds her inside. The zombie's vast strength nearly yanks Kirby out of the car. Oliver's eyes meet the zombie's and Oliver sees . . . fear in them. An emotion he recognizes as human. It's the last thing he expected to see—and he has no idea what it means.

But then the van lurches and the zombie lets go.

As the van speeds ahead, the zombie holds on to the side of the vehicle, then climbs up on the roof. The heat of the creature seeps through the metal.

"What are you doing, Kirby?" her mother demands. Oliver and Kirby just look at each other. But there's no time for an argument, so Oliver shoves his nose into his notes.

"Dad, get ready!" says Oliver. "There's a big swerve coming up, the water's gonna go to the left—you gun the engine to the *right*, okay?"

"Yeah!" says Oliver's dad, loud. Then, to himself, taking a deep breath, "Okay . . ."

Out the open door, Oliver sees the whitewater gushing hard to the left. And in the water, he sees an impossible face. Bloodless skin, watery eyes, mouth sluicing water as it emerges—

What is this? Oliver is so fixated in horror he nearly forgets why he's here, and warns his father of the upcoming left turn a second too late.

"Dad, now!!"

The car strains to mount the natural bank of the temporary river, but Oliver's distraction ruined their timing. The wheels spin and spin—

The engine sputters, and fails—

It's not going to make it. Their one chance slips away—

In an agonizing slow motion, the car slides back into the river and is pulled forward again by the hungry rapids. Then the car slowly stops, then gets pulled forward again, in the steely grasp of the amphibious undead. Heading straight for the valley's swollen, deep river . . .

"Abandon ship," says Oliver.

"And go where?" says Oliver's mom.

The water around them is too fast, too powerful. As the van swings to face forward, all the water rushing downhill starts to surge in through the jammed-open sliding door—

—And in the surge is something else, too. Something covered in squelching, slippery sludge, with a trail of snail slime coming from its muscle-bound mouth.

"Roof!" says Kirby. She pushes out on the spiderwebbed back window and climbs through it as what can only be described as the new face of the zombie menace pushes inside the minivan. Looking in its inky eyes is like looking into the depths of the sea.

36

Nix will always remember the look the girl gave him as she reached out her arm toward him, pulling him from the grasp of the floodwater.

As the girl climbs up on the roof of the minivan with him, followed by her brother and her mother, their eyes meet once more. Nix's mouth opens to speak, but the mother thinks it's an attack and leaps in front of her.

Nix wants to reach out and push her aside, but he struggles to stop himself. Remembering what Regina told him about how *not* to make friends.

Seeing the surge of the rapids, sensing what circles them, he knows this will be his only chance to make a different choice.

And then. Inside the van, a boy screams. A man bellows in fury. Two human bodies launch through the window, into the water. It's a race to the shoreline, with two murky patches in the water stalking after them.

Nix doesn't watch how it ends. Because there's another creature coming out of the van, too. Up onto the roof. It is a creature unlike any even Nix has seen before.

It is more than a zombie. It is another stage of zombie, Nix realizes: As humans become zombies, so do zombies become the creature emerging

205

from the water. With skin that's translucent, showing the impossibly cold, sapphire-blue blood inside. With eyes as dark as the water that pulls you under, to the depths you'll never again escape. Slime covers it, and it oozes with a squelching sound. And as it reaches the roof, Nix looks at the terrified girl and knows that it is his turn.

He tackles the creature, and pushes it off the car. Water flashes to steam as Nix lands in the rapids, leaving him cold. Powerless. Trapped.

The last thing Nix can remember is using his final strength to shove the minivan to the edge of the water—

And then there is nothing.

37

LIFE AND UNDEATH

"What *was* that?" Oliver asks. A safe distance back from the rushing floodwater's edge, he leans heavily against a tree that's a little bit less muddy than the rest. Beside him is his mother, holding both her children tight. She tends to Kirby's injury, wincing a little at the red patch where the zombie's fingers held her tight. Farther down the bank, they can see Oliver's father pulling Del from the water and sheltering him in the same way.

"Is it over?" Oliver asks.

No one answers him for a moment.

And then, in his pocket, he feels a buzz. His phone is ringing.

"Hello?" he says. The voice on the other end sounds like it's underwater.

There's another buzzing. In Oliver's *other* pocket.

He hits the green button to take the call. But before he can even ask who it is, there's a girl's voice barking out his name. "Oliver Wachs! It's Regina Herrera."

"Regina? Are you okay?"

"I need your help, Ollie."

"What's going on?"

What she tells him is unbelievable.

But at this point . . . he'll believe anything.

As Regina explains, Oliver's eyes dart to the rushing water with new fear.

Far down in the valley, Chief Wachs and her team have mopped up most of the zombie mess. When she sees Oliver's name come up on her screen, she answers it instantly. "Hey, Ollie. Is it urgent?"

"Emergency!" Oliver's voice comes through the phone. She can hear his breath, shallow and fast. "Aunt C, you need to listen. We need to send out a Dusk Alert. To the whole county. Everyone near a body of water needs to get to higher ground, *right now*."

"Oliver, slow down," says Chief Wachs. "What's going on?"

"You need to send an alert, and get everyone to high ground. *They're in the water now.*"

Her head swivels around, looking at the engorged river just beside her, seeing nothing. "What's in the water?"

"Zombies are in the water."

"Zombies."

"Listen to me. I saw one. This isn't a prank, this is serious stuff. Life and undeath stuff. Superchillers don't work on them. To these guys supercooled water is *fuel*. It just makes them *stronger*."

Chief Wachs pauses, taking in everything she's being told.

She looks at the two freeze trucks pouring a steady gush of supercooled water on every single extinguished zombie in sight, and a shiver goes through her.

"Hello?" Oliver asks. "Are you still there?"

"Yeah. Ollie, I—"

"Aunt C," says Oliver. "Please. I saw them with my own eyes. People need to *move*. Right now. Get to high ground. Away from any deep water."

Chief Wachs looks at the engorged river once more, with fresh respect for the power that lies in its depths.

"I can't," she says, numbly.

"What?" Oliver asks.

"I can't send an alert from here. We lost the mobile command center. It's gone. And the only other place I can send a Dusk Alert from is the call center at headquarters, which has been evacuated, and the roads are unusable right now."

"I can get to headquarters," says Oliver. "I'm close right now."

"Ollie, no. No way."

Sitting on the banks of what's now become only a trickling creek, Oliver mentally maps a route to the zombie brigade headquarters. "If you can tell me how to send an alert, I can get there on foot to do it," says Oliver.

As Oliver speaks into the phone, he can feel his mother's head turn. "Ollie?" she says. "Speakerphone. Now."

Oliver sees she's very serious and does what she asks. "Come on, Aunt C," says Oliver.

Chief Wachs thinks about this for a long moment, as Oliver explains everything to his mom and dad.

"I'll go," says Oliver's dad.

"You still need me to find a safe path," says Oliver, holding up his notebook.

"Fine. Yes. Do it, Ollie." Chief Wachs's heavy, serious voice comes through the speakerphone. "Be safe."

38

THE EVER-CHANGING WORLD

Step after step, Oliver digs his feet into the muck.

It wasn't easy convincing his mother to let them split up, but the reality was that it made no sense to risk more lives than they had to. Mom needed to help Kirby and Del get to high ground, where they'd be safe from the treacherous waters. And Oliver needed to help . . . the world.

Desperate times call for desperate heroes.

No one knows the paths like I do, he promised his mother. *I can make it there and send out the alert.*

What he hadn't added was: *If any of the paths still exist.*

Lungs struggling, heart past its limit, Oliver uses all his knowledge of the terrain to find any clear way to the zombie brigade's headquarters. Again and again, he runs up against obstacles, and it takes all his experience and creativity to navigate around them.

"Let's go, Dad!" Oliver calls out as his father struggles to keep up.

They're not moving fast enough, Oliver knows. Not nearly fast enough. Every moment he spends keeping himself safe now is an awful risk to the people he's out here to save.

Across Redwood, the water from the storm is pooling in larger and larger amounts. Thick with debris, logs, trash, flooded cars, and the putrid corpses of extinguished zombies.

Digging even deeper, hearing the seconds tick on in his mind, he keeps laser focused on the path ahead of him, and on the notebook in his hands that's even now just barely accurate enough to use to navigate the changed, eroded hillside. With all the toppled trees and flooded areas, the GPS on Oliver's phone is no help. Nothing but a taunting reminder of how slow they're moving.

Caught looking at the phone screen, it's an unwelcome shock when he finds his foot slipping—

"No no no!" Oliver shouts, sliding through the mud like it's a skateboard he's balanced atop. He reaches backward, searching for his balance, but there's no traction.

Uh-oh.

The ground and his body connect with a bone-jarring impact. In a daze, Oliver realizes he had *just* enough nimbleness to land on his butt, and not his head, as he skidded to a stop on the far side of the mud-slicked street.

"Oliver!" his dad shouts, sprinting to his side.

"I'm okay."

Rising to his feet again, Oliver looks around to get his bearings, but all he sees is more mud and icy patches, and minefields of debris strewn across his path through the zombie-damaged ruins of Redwood.

Nothing is familiar.

Nothing makes sense.

That's when he sees them.

"Dad, look!"

Oliver's father looks where he points, and sees: "Carole? Danny!"

It's Del's parents. Sheltered beside a culvert full of rushing water, unaware of the danger.

Oliver sprints toward them. But something's wrong.

Neither of them is moving.

"Dad, help!!" Oliver shouts. Oliver doesn't know what to do; all his hope is souring.

Oliver's father arrives out of breath, but he wastes no time in testing Del's parents for signs of life. "They're not dead," he says. "But we can't leave them here."

As Oliver's dad keeps giving first aid to Del's parents, Oliver slowly gets to his feet.

"Dad." Oliver and his father exchange a serious look. "They need you. You stay. Let me finish this."

Oliver's father looks horrified. "No, Oliver."

"This is my home turf, Dad. Please. Trust me."

Oliver's dad looks around, seeking any other answer.

"It's like you said, Dad. We're living with consequences of past actions. We can't change that; all we can do is deal with them. One at a time."

Oliver's dad gives Oliver a strange look. A hopeful look. "I trust you, Ollie," his dad says, pulling him into a hug that goes on for a long time.

And then Oliver is moving again. Alone.

"Keep it together, Wachs," he says under his ragged breaths, pulling out his green notebook and looking for a landmark. Unfortunately, his fall in the mud has been disastrous for the notebook. All the pages are translucent, sticking together, tearing apart. It's useless. All that's legible are the seven words on the cover:

"*One foot in front of the other,*" he says, with no choice but to believe in himself and keep going. It feels like the world itself is coming apart—rearranging itself according to the terrible, unnatural pressure acting on it.

He takes a step, acting totally confident and feeling absolutely lost.

He takes a second step, thinking about his mom, his sister, his aunt, his dad, Del, and everyone else out there right now counting on him. And he plants his foot firmly, proudly—

There's a little tiny twinge in his ankle, but he ignores it, seeing a tree with a sparkling ribbon tied around its trunk.

"No way!" he says, recognizing it. "Our trail marker."

Suddenly, the dread in Oliver's mind lifts, and it's replaced with a memory of the neighborhood kids all working together to mark the trails that Oliver used to escape during Manhunt. He doesn't need his notebook or GPS if he's got the trail markers. Plus? He's a lot closer than he thought. He starts building up speed, taking a third step, and a fourth—looking around the hill ahead of him, he can see the top floor of zombie brigade headquarters! But on that fourth step, as he plants his foot and it takes all his weight, there's a terrible, blinding pain that lances up his leg, all the way to his brain.

A ringing sound fills his ears, but he pushes onward through it. Oliver grabs a fallen tree branch and puts his weight on it, like it's a crutch, as he continues toward the building that he can see over the next hill.

The ringing sound continues, and gets louder, but he keeps focused on the trail. Following its markers: paint on a curb, barely visible with all the mud. Two straight lines of rocks, parallel, on either side of the trail that leads past the hill . . .

Adrenaline pulls him onward. More and more of zombie brigade headquarters sprawls out in front of Oliver. Floor by floor, it grows.

But then, as the ground level comes into view, Oliver's gut flips.

There's flooding everywhere. Even worse, the water is *moving*. Churning.

As Oliver watches, a twenty-foot-tall zombie with translucent blue skin and white lips *surges* from the water, like a tidal wave. Perched on its shoulder is the wrecked remains of the top story of someone's house. A bedroom set shakes loose as it roars and sets to its hunt. Around its legs, a quartet of smaller, slimy zombies skitter, and as one they all slam their bodies into the side of the building like a battering ram. Quickly losing energy, they retreat to the water again, but a moment later there's another surge and another impact.

Oliver can only gawk. The brigade's headquarters is under siege.

Again, the giant zombie launches itself at the building. It seems to shrink a little more after each assault . . . at least until it returns to the water. Mentally, Oliver makes a note of this: This kind of zombie can't come onto dry land for very long, it seems?

Oliver is so hypnotized that he doesn't notice that something's behind him. Coming up fast. A hand clasps his shoulder—

He screams and spins around.

"Oliver Wachs, I've been calling you. Like fifty times!" hisses Regina Herrera, eyes wide in extreme agitation.

"Regina, what are you . . . ?"

"Figured you could use some help," says Regina, with a shrug.

Oliver doesn't know what to say, so he just wraps her in a hug.

She hugs him back and almost knocks him over.

"You're hurt?" she realizes, seeing his makeshift crutch.

"I'm fine," Oliver insists. "How'd you find me?"

"Tracked your phone. Well. *My* phone. Not important whose phone it is, I guess," she says, sounding kind of embarrassed. "After we hung up and there was no new Dusk Alert, I got really nervous something went wrong. Especially when I couldn't get hold of you. So. I started tracking your location, deduced where you were headed. Got here fast as I could."

"Wow." Oliver looks impressed. "Is it just you, or . . . ?"

"My mother is fully occupied trying to stop her boss from launching any more Cloudbusters, and Joule's safe with her mom at high ground. They're texting everyone in their contacts to get to safety as fast as they can. But we *need* to send that alert. What's the situation?"

"There's something very big between us and the warning system," Oliver tells her, gesturing to what's plain before her eyes. "Got any ideas?"

Along every side of the building, there's a trench that can be flooded in case of a zombie wave, to help the brigade fight them off. But the engineers who built the trench never imagined something like today—a situation where a trench filled with water is incredibly dangerous.

Regina and Oliver hunker down and think.

"Why are they here?" says Regina.

"That's a good question. Better question: How do we lure them away, so we can get inside?"

"Oh man," says Regina. "Look up on the roof."

Oliver scans the roof, not seeing anything strange. "What am I looking at?" he asks.

"Well, that's a tower full of supercooled water, isn't it? To fill the freeze trucks?"

"I think so. Why?"

Regina looks amazed. "This whole building is kind of like a huge super-chiller, isn't it?"

"Regina, clock's ticking. Get to the point."

"Come with me!" says Regina, standing up and heading straight to the front door of the building. Right in the open, where any zombie could see her.

Oliver doesn't chase after her. "Regina?! What are you *doing*?"

Behind her, the huge zombie and four only slightly smaller ones slam against the building, bringing down a cascade of bricks and cement.

"Come on, Ollie!" she calls out, dancing around out in the open. "Clock's ticking!"

Cautiously, Oliver starts to follow her. Keeping as low to the ground as he can on his makeshift crutch.

To Oliver's astonishment, the zombies are totally ignoring the humans in their midst. As Oliver hobbles toward Regina, she goes back to help him, and they enter the brigade headquarters together.

Every few seconds, the whole building shakes, as the zombies surge again and again.

"Thanks, Regina," he says, with admiration. "How'd you guess they'd leave us alone?"

"These zombies *love* supercooled water. They must be attracted to it. The whole building is basically a huge zombie lure."

Again, the building shakes, and plaster showers down from the ceiling. Far deeper in the building, there's a long series of creaks and groans of straining metal.

"They really want it, don't they?" Oliver marvels.

"Let's do this and get outta here fast," says Regina.

Oliver nods. "Yeah, that's a really good idea."

That's when Oliver looks down the hall and sees a flicker of movement. He grabs Regina's wrist and whispers. "Regina? I don't think we're alone in here. We're just here to send a message. We get in and get out."

Regina nods. "You're the one who knows the system. Lead the way."

"Up here," says Oliver, hopping up the stairs to the second floor, where the 9-6-6 call center is usually abuzz with activity. Today, it's eerily still.

But the surges outside keep coming, every ten seconds. Like the building's heartbeat.

And now there are footsteps inside the building, too.

"Here," says Oliver, making his way to an open office and turning on the computer.

As it starts up, the lights flicker.

"How long is this gonna take?" says Regina, nervously keeping an eye out.

"I've never done it before," says Oliver, tapping the keyboard experimentally. "But how hard can it be to send a text?"

The lights go out a bit longer with the next impact. Regina's eyes meet Oliver's nervously as the computer beeps, ready for a command.

"Working on it!" Oliver says, pulling out the green notebook where he wrote his aunt's instructions. "Oh no," he says. The mud-caked notebook is far past readability.

"Oliver . . ."

"I remember, I remember," Oliver says, trying to reassure her. Trying to convince himself . . .

As Regina watches and keeps her eyes peeled, the lights go fully out in the whole building. In the darkness, a vast metal *screech* follows the zombies' latest smash against the building, followed by a huge, hollow *boom!* that rumbles through Oliver's legs, up into his chest.

From outside the building, a moan that sounds more like long peal of thunder reaches them.

"So, what happens if a tower full of supercooled water lands on that zombie?" Oliver asks.

Before Regina comes up with an answer to this, the phone in Oliver's pocket buzzes with the Dusk Alert signal.

39

THE END

"Never thought I'd be so glad to hear that awful sound," Oliver says, taking out the phone to show Regina.

DUSK ALERT: Get to higher ground. Their are zombies in the water.

Reading the message, Regina looks like she wants to say something, but she bites it back. "Okay, okay. Okay."

"What's the problem?"

"No problem," says Regina. "I just . . . you messed up your 'their' and 'there'—"

"What! No, I didn't," Oliver says, looking at his phone. Oliver's face goes red with embarrassment. "Oh man. How many people did this just go out to?"

The foundation of the building shakes like there's a tremor. "You want to stay and send another message?" Regina asks.

"Nope. I'm good." Oliver doesn't sound very sure of this. But just at that moment, from deeper in the building, there's a sound of something crashing through the halls, letting out a terrible, hungry moan as its footsteps thunder forward.

Regina grabs Oliver and ducks under his arm to support his weight and help him get out the door. As they hobble down the stairs, the door leading outside seems to stretch and stretch farther and farther away.

"Regina? You gotta run for it. I'll only slow you down," Oliver says, gesturing to his leg.

"I'm not leaving you," Regina says, hiking him up a little so his weight's almost all on her as they barge into the building lobby, with bricks and plaster falling all around them.

They pause, under cover, as water cascades across the floor, soaking everything.

"Go," Oliver pleads with Regina.

"On three. *Together*."

She counts, holding Oliver tight.

"Go! Now!" she bellows, and sprints for the door. Her strength is surprising to Oliver.

But he forces himself to run alongside her. Oliver's feet stiffen in the terrible cold as he splashes through the icy water from the supercooling tower. He screams, in equal parts pain and determination, as the water catches up with them and overtakes them.

And then they're outside. The sun is bright on Oliver's face, and the ground is squishy under his half-numb, frostbitten feet. A wild cheer erupts from

Oliver's throat and he slumps over to the ground as Regina ducks out from under his arm.

"Wait here," Regina says, racing away.

"Where are you going?" he calls after her.

And as he does, the sun is thrown into shadow.

The air gets cold.

As Oliver looks up, he sees five giant-sized zombies with translucent blue skin and a more intense hunger than ever. Towering. Terrible.

There's nowhere left for him to run, but he climbs to his feet anyway, hobbling away as best he can.

"Grab on, Oliver!" Regina calls out, zooming toward Oliver on a motorized, one-wheel skateboard. She shoots right through the legs of the largest zombie and Oliver *leaps*!

For a moment, he's in midair, and then . . .

"Gotcha!" Regina crows in triumph. He can feel her struggling for balance, and still she keeps the skateboard motor churning at top speed. "Okay, Ollie. Your turn. Get us out of here."

Oliver thinks fast, but he's losing focus. All the struggle to get here has left him empty. Tired. So cold that it's almost warm.

"Hey! Stay awake!" says Regina, as she feels his grasp slipping. She elbows him in the kidney and the pain brings Oliver to a groggy, angry awareness.

"I'm awake." Oliver looks behind them. The zombies continue to chase.

Something about them is drawing his keen eye. Something that's hard to pin down.

But then it hits him.

"Uphill, Regina. Higher ground."

"You got it," she says, zigzagging back and forth to get their overheating little motor to keep climbing the steep hill.

Behind them, the zombies don't turn aside. They bear straight down on Regina and Oliver. But even as they gain ground, they start to get visibly *smaller* than before.

"Oliver, which way now?"

"Keep going. This is gonna work."

"I can't keep going. It's a dead end! Left or right?!"

"Straight, don't turn! Keep going," says Oliver. "Trust me!"

Regina swallows hard and zooms forward. Oliver can see the lip of the valley ahead, a sheer cliff that tumbles back down the other side . . .

The zombies are getting smaller fast now. They're ten-footers. Then nine. They make a final *lunge* forward—

We're gonna make it, Oliver thinks, feeling a warmth blossom inside him.

He feels himself falling, and doesn't stop himself.

And then he doesn't feel anything at all.

———

At the lip of the valley, heart racing as she looks at the steep fall ahead, Regina feels like she's about to be sick.

She looks back, prepared for the worst.

But what she sees are five regular-sized zombies, exhausted and struggling to claw through the mud toward her.

They're drying out like jellyfish do. When all the water in them is gone,
there's so little left.

But her moment of victory is cut very short, because Oliver Wachs is
blue-lipped, his eyes half-closed.

"Oliver!" she calls out.

She bends over him, rubbing his arms and legs hard to warm him up.

"You did it, Regina," he says weakly.

"We did it." Regina feels an anger rising inside her. And she focuses on
Oliver—pushing that heat toward him, with all the willpower she has.

Oliver sucks in a breath, surprised. He looks at her, wide-eyed.

"What are you doing?"

"You are my friend and I'm not just gonna let you freeze," she says,
embarrassed and determined.

To Regina's surprise, the mud starts to crack and dry out.

Oliver feels his arms and legs light up in pins and needles. Every nerve in
his body erupts in pain. But it anchors him there, in that moment. Alive.

"You with me, Wachs?" she asks nervously.

Oliver nods wearily. "Where are we going?"

"Let's just sit here a minute, okay?"

He nods.

"Okay." She just slumps down on the ground beside Oliver. The ground under them seems to pinwheel, blurry with speed. Only when they look up does the queasy feeling ease.

Together, Regina and Oliver stare up into the sky.

On every hilltop around them, the rest of the citizens of Redwood join them, one by one.

40

OFF THE MAP

A couple days later, Regina goes for a walk with Joule.

Joule is still in California because nothing is working quite right in the wake of the Rogue Wave's destruction. The Herreras' own house was destroyed, so Regina and her mother returned to the Artises' home, who were happy to take them in. Regina's mom is still livid that she went out to help Oliver. But she trusts Joule to keep an eye on her daughter.

And Regina, of course, wants to make the most of her remaining time with Joule.

"I don't want you to leave, Joule," Regina confesses.

Joule wraps her in a hug. "You are a good friend," she says, pushing the words deep into Regina's mind.

"We'll talk online," Regina promises.

Regina knows she'll be sad to see Joule go. But she also knows her investigations into HumaniTeam will continue. Before this, she was mostly concerned with what damage Project Coloma had done. Now she knows it goes much deeper than that. Deeper, and more dangerous.

It's a potentially lethal assignment.

But that's not going to stop Regina.

She doesn't want anyone else to have to live through what she's just lived through.

And she doesn't want anyone else to have to endure what she imagines Nix has endured, either.

———————

"This is it, huh?" As Joule and her mother make their last stop on the way to the airport, there's a vast feeling of . . . mourning that floods her entire body.

The Santifer orchard has been completely rearranged by calamity.

It's not the place that it used to be. It's a little wilder now. A little uncertain about its purpose.

But this hasn't diminished the place, Joule decides.

Whatever the orchard makes of itself, it is precious beyond measure.

And she is grateful to have been part of this place, where trees pull water from the sky without it ever needing to fall as rain. Where fruit grows better than anywhere else in the world. A place she is connected to by something more deeply rooted in her than her heart even understands.

She releases all her feelings, all her love, in a single wish. Her eyes blur with tears that don't fall, and her throat tightens against a sob that fades—

The world is green, and gold, and moves far too quickly.

OLIVER, JOULE, AND REGINA SURVIVED THE MOST RECENT
ATTACKS, BUT ZOMBIE SEASON HAS ONLY JUST BEGUN.
THE ADVENTURE CONTINUES WITH

ZOMBIE SEASON

BOOK 2

WITH REDWOOD DESTROYED, THE SURVIVORS ARE DOING THEIR BEST
TO ADJUST TO THEIR NEW REALITY. BUT A NEW THREAT IS LURKING IN
THE SHADOWS—AN ENEMY THAT NO ONE BELIEVED EXISTED. ONE
THAT WAS JUST WAITING FOR THE RIGHT MOMENT TO STRIKE . . .

ARE YOU READY FOR
ZOMBIE SEASON?

Oliver, Joule, and Regina helped avert disaster in Redwood, but their problems have only begun. What secrets will Regina discover at the HumaniTeam headquarters? And what will she do once she learns the shocking truth about the zombies' origin? Regina needs YOUR help and she's waiting for you at her hidden base where you'll be able to:

Fight zombies and collect supplies.

Read top secret files and uncover dangerous secrets.

And much more!

PLAY NOW!

JOIN THE FIGHT AT
SCHOLASTIC.COM/ZOMBIESEASON

ACKNOWLEDGMENTS

This story has been a wonderful adventure for me from the start, and I'm eternally grateful for everyone in my life who has been a part of this book's journey, and mine.

From the very beginning, David Levithan was there to bring uncanny clarity and perspective to the endeavor. And in every twist and turn, Mallory Kass's steady editorial guidance and constant inspiration have imbued this zombie-filled world with life.

I will never forget how this book has made me feel reconnected to my community amidst pandemic distancing, and to everyone who contributed to this project—my deepest gratitude. Thank you to Ellie Berger. Thank you to the Scholastic sales team. Thank you to Rachel Feld, Erin Berger, Seale Ballanger, and Lia Ferrone. Thank you to Melissa Schirmer and Stephanie Yang. Thank you to Jalen Garcia-Hall.

To Gavin Brown, Andrea Lowry and Mario Chuman: Joule, Oliver and Regina have no idea how lucky they are to have you at their back when they're facing down zombie hordes. Thank you to Julie Amitie, Katie Dutton,